Better Days

By

Bertrand Brown

This book is a work of fiction. Names, characters, places, and incidents either are products of the author's imagination or are used fictitiously. Any resemblance to actual persons, living or dead, events, or locales is entirely coincidental.

ISBN-13 978-1511596718

Ally and the Yellow Butterfly

Nowadays Alicia's thoughts often drifted to those nights when she was eight or nine years old. Those days of innocence seemed so very long ago. She could easily recall playing outside at night when the sun would go off somewhere to sleep and the moon took its place while it rested. And she knew that it wouldn't be long before she too would have to leave her friends and go in and do the same. They were friends then with all the innocence of children. Hidden agendas were somewhere down the road and everything was as it seemed. And as long as Eunice and Ernest stood there talking to the neighbors she could run and jump and chase lightning bugs with the rest of the kids. She had her jar and would snap the top on tightly. Daddy had poked holes in the top so the tiny bugs could breathe and she couldn't remember happier times.

Nowadays she would look back and remember those days as if it were yesterday and smile. Life had changed so much since then. Things had been so simple. She had always been daddy's little girl but as the years went on she traded daddy's love in for other men's love but those men--if you wanted to call them men paled in comparison and she had yet to find another man out there that treated her the way daddy did.

Daddy never asked her for anything. He was too intent on spoiling her. Oh, he might have required her to do well in school but then he never had to ask that. She prided herself on being a good girl and making her parents proud by doing everything precisely and by the book. As far as her parents went there was no question of how much they adored their little Alicia. And Alicia wanted for little except maybe a brother or sister to share her life with but oh well that was out of her hands.

And as life would have it little Alicia grew up. Before she knew it she was a woman. Her body matured accordingly. Thick with a fine, round ass and breasts that caused even old men to take a second look Alicia liked the attention and dressed to accentuate her blessings. Before she knew it she had garnered the attention of more than just one boy. All professed their love for her but unlike daddy their love wasn't innocent and unconditional. Sure, they all professed their undying love and devotion for her. But unlike daddy it didn't come without a cost. They all wanted something from her. All of them. And it was always the same thing.

At first, Alicia naively believed them to be sincere in their love for her. Her phone rang constantly and some even came by to visit. They took her out and laughed and joked and in those uncomfortable silences each professed their undying love for her. But in the end it was always the same. And after they'd convinced her that they loved her and wanted to be with her forever and a day she would give in to their desires and after much trepidation allow them to physically Alicia love her.

In the days and months that followed after she conceded in allowing them to grope and feel and sex her til they had had their fill of her body her phone would stop ringing.

She could recall her very first boyfriend. She'd been head over heels in love with Greg Johnson and he was the first man the first she allowed to reach in and touch her inner sanctum, and he had been the first man she'd let penetrate her heart and her soul and with that reluctantly came her body. But it was okay. They were in love. They'd been together close to two years and she couldn't have been happier. She was in love and things couldn't have been much better. He filled the void of her being an only child. He was the brother and sister she never had. He was her best friend and confidante. He was her lover. But more than anything he was her friend. And he was in every sense a man. He worked at J&L steel mills, made a good salary and had his own car. After a couple of years they were no longer just boyfriend and girlfriend but like an old married couple. They were compatible and for once Alicia felt complete and whole.

Then there was that night she'd gone to the Speakeasy in New Brighton after some friends had taken her to the Earth, Wind & Fire. It was her eighteenth birthday and all was right with the world or so it seemed. She'd only recently been accepted at the tiny state school not far from home and she was far enough from mommy and daddy at the small state college not far from her home in Beaver, Pennsylvania to have some independence. And though she would have much rather gone to D.C. or Atlanta but the tiny school served her well for right now.

Not far from Eunice and Ernest and close enough that she could still see Greg on weekends it was for all intents and purposes ideal. In truth life couldn't get much better and this particular night Alicia and her girls toasted her coming of age and all being right with the world. That was until her baby, her sweetie, the love of her life and best friend Greg Johnson walked in with his handsome, chocolate brown self looking just as fine as he wanted to be. She wondered how life could get any better. Up until that point she hadn't noticed that he was being accompanied by a woman. All she saw was Greg. And then just as quickly Alicia's world came tumbling down. All that had been good was now bad. She had never imagined a hurt so deep, so painful, so severe. She was numb, in a state of shock and could barely hear the muffled voices around her but had a hard time distinguishing the voices or the people associated with them. Rage encompassed her whole being. She could only see red and was intent on returning the hurt she was now feeling but when she started to rise she felt her girl's hands restraining her.

"He ain't worth it, Alicia," she heard them say faintly.

The voices in her head were quite different. They spoke of her undying love and devotion for Greg. Up until now she had never felt this loved or loved anyone this much in her life. And he had taken it all for granted. How could he do this to her? How could he cheat on her? How could he betray her like this? Wasn't it just yesterday when he told her how he would do anything for her? How could he hurt her like this? She was angry. Bitter. She would never ever be duped so easily again. Never. The brick she threw through his car window that gave Jazmine Sullivan the inspiration for her song, 'Bust the Windows Out Your Car' helped little to mask her hurt.

In the days that followed Alicia would sit on the edge of her bed holding her teddy bear and wonder if her forever and a day was somehow different for her than it was for them. But not to be outdone she would give it the old college try and step right back up to bat. After all, Hattye and Ernest had been married eighteen or nineteen years and sure it wasn't perfect but then what marriage was. The bottom line was that they loved each other and supported each other during the highs and lows and whatever else came in between but never had she seen her parents deliberately hurt each other. Life may have taken its toll on them as life often does but never had she seen them deliberately cause the other hardship and all she wanted was to pattern their model. Leaving for college would be a good thing.

The only problem is she couldn't seem to find a guy that had a Hattye and Ernest to model their relationships after. Still, Alicia didn't give up falling in love time-after-time only to come up with the same outcome. But for the time being se would put love on the backburner. For now she'd be content to meet a guy enjoy his company with little expectations other than to that certain young man to jump out of being that typical guy and to ride in on his white horse swoop down, pick her up and ride away with her into the sunset and make her his queen forever.

Starting college she was surprise at how different things were from the tiny, lily white town of Beaver she'd grown up in and though the small town of California, Pennsylvania was a far cry from New York City or Washington, D.C. it was like a homecoming of sorts. Never before in her life had she seen so many beautiful Black men in one place and se soon became swept up in school and the different on campus organizations. And at the end of the day when her studies were complete she went about the business of socializing which meant getting to know the people to know on campus.

At the time, in the late seventies, there was a very popular soap opera on television called Peyton Place, a very small community wrought with scandal, sex and gossip. California State College mirrored this and at the end of the day when the business of education was completed and the yard as it was called in those days Alicia came alive young men would call to check and make sure their girlfriends were in their dorm rooms and on their way to sleep before making that second call to let the single women know the coast was clear. Alicia was on the second wave.

By this time Alicia, had for the most part given up on men or the idea that men served any purpose other than sex or that they had any concept of faithfulness and she like the other single chicks waited for the lights to go out before starting her journey after hours. They called it 'Creepin' after the very popular Luther Vandross song. And creep she did with no concern for the woman she'd be hurting. After all, hadn't some woman done the same thing with her Greg only a month or so before. Girlfriends better keep their men in check was her new philosophy when it came to other's relationships. She had no sympathy and no concern about some other woman's love life. She had nothing to do with that. This was the new Alicia. She was going to do her and it was up to whoever to watch their back.

In the back of her mind, she still considered what Hattye and Ernest had as special but for some reason it didn't seem like it was meant for her. They'd been born in a different world and Ernest wasn't the typical brother. He was true to his namesake and earnest in his endeavors. He saw one woman by the name of Hattye and was true to her and her alone. But this new Blackman was neither earnest nor sincere and no matter how much you committed and did to support these new Black men in their endeavors they were always on the prowl seeking something different, something better, some strange. Recognizing this Alicia took on a similar philosophy and crept from dorm to dorm meeting and sleeping with those she found attractive in one way or another. And as dorm doors cracked and blinds went up and young boys who had no concept of what it meant to be men chattered away about who they had last night Alicia's name was always at the top of the list.

When the young women on campus heard the rumors they became incensed that the new girl had had their man while they slept while Alicia would only smile and say 'Don't sleep girlfriend.' And like Peyton Place the word spread.

When I arrived on campus in 1981 fresh out of the Marines I was like most young Black men in awe of the fresh new meat on campus and spent my first semester seeing how many of these fine young Black girls I could have the pleasure of spending a night or two with. My libido on high I cruised the campus daily looking for potential prospects and had all but exhausted the supply of single ladies when I happened to bump into Alicia who by now had come a long way from innocently chasing lightning bugs.

I at once was intrigued by her hard exterior and was curious as to how anyone so young could be so mean and bitter. After awhile I was awarded a smile and wondered what lay beneath her cold exterior. When I asked to see her later that day I was surprised when she readily agreed but agree she did. I can't recollect what we did on our first date but I enjoyed her company and found that beneath the cold exterior she was a warm, classy, thoughtful young woman.

Born worlds apart we shared the same values and both came from good homes and suddenly my need to bed down every woman on campus was cut short. In Alicia I found everything I'd been missing and although we slept together after the second or third date that is not what I found most intriguing. We talked considerably and I was surprised at how much we had in common. To me and out of all the young women I had come to meet in my first year on campus here was the keeper.

Still, I had no idea what had preceded and hardly cared. I was several years older than most of my colleagues and I suppose growing up in New York City had a lot to do with how I went about doing things but one of the first things I was to learn when it came to women was that you never kiss and tell--well that is if you're a man. That however, was not the way it was with these small town wannabe men here in Peyton Place.

One day, not long after meeting Alicia my homeboy and I were preparing to go to the cafeteria for dinner and for some reason Derek felt compelled to knock on everyone's door to see if they wanted to join us. This usually took fifteen or twenty minutes and when we were finally on our way we usually had a crew of ten or twelve of the fellows. I guess it was a Philly thing as most of the brothers were from Philadelphia and were affiliated with some type of social organization called MIAKA, (Men Interested in AKA's).

In any case, Alicia was an AKA, (the elite Black women's sorority on campus), and the first room we stopped by was this brother who Derek insisted on me meeting.

"B. You're going to love this brother. He's an older cat and he's cool like that. I don't mean like he's older. I mean like he's mature. You know he's into things that most of these younger kids ain't into."

And with that he knocked on Darren Devoe's dorm room door. They shook hands and bumped chests and we were invited in.

"Darren this is the brother I was telling you about. B. this is Darren. Y'all remind me so much of each other I just had to introduce you. B.'s from New York and cool as hell."

I smiled. Everyone was cool as hell to Derek. Darren and I shook hands and I looked at the brother who didn't appear cool to me at all as he sat there acting like he was Ernie Isley or Jimi Hendrix trying to pluck away and get something to resemble a song from his guitar. His next words hit me like a ton of bricks.

"Oh, yeah. I heard about you. You're that new cat on campus."

I shook my head to see where he was going with this. Never looking up from the bad notes he was playing on his guitar he continued.

"I hear you're talking to A.B.?"

I smiled thinking that the next few words could make us lifelong friends or the most hated of enemies. All my friends had commented on my talking to her. And all had been appropriate for the most part. Derek had been the first and simply said 'Alicia's a good choice man. Most of these bitches are scandalous but A.B.'s a nice girl.'

Derek being a good friend was honest, loyal, and trustworthy and his endorsement meant a lot. But I'd just met this kid and his next words would make or break him as far as I was concerned. Fact was that I was crazy about her despite what anyone said but you'd best not say or even think anything derogatory about her. Most of the time I heard things about her weight or something about her having a big ass but I took those as compliments and would simply counter with 'I like that about her. It's just more for me to hold on to.' Truth was she was beautiful to me. Oh, she had her flaws as we all do. She was spoiled and could be mean as a rattle snake on a hot, summer afternoon but I quickly came to ignore that part of her and concentrate on her positives and she had plenty of those. She had an easy laugh and had the biggest heart of anyone I'd ever met and would go to the ends of the earth if she loved you. And it was already obvious that she or I should say we were falling head over heels in love although she would hardly admit it.

"So, I hear you're talking to A.B." he repeated.

"Yeah," I answered wondering now where this motherfucker was going with this shit. My friends could comment on me talking to her and dating her but I didn't know this cat.

"Oh yeah. That's good," he said now looking up at me. "You'll like her. She gives good head."

Derek must have known. Grabbing me by the arm he pushed me towards the door. Together we had been in several dorm fights and one or two in the cafeteria over dumb shit just like this.

Once outside, he apologized.

"Sorry B. I thought he was cool. I didn't know he was gonna come off like that."

"H's a little bitch. What dude kisses and tells. Why the fuck would he ask me if I was seeing her then tell me she sucked his dick. Who does that? You told me the brother was cool. He ain't nothing but a little bitch. I expect a woman to do something like that but where I'm from your ass'll get stomped doing some shit like that. I should have stomped his little punk ass. Little bitch!!" I screamed hoping he would hear me.

"I'm sorry B."

I never spoke to Darren Devoe again. But I had some close friends who lived on the edge of campus who told me quite bluntly. 'I hope you know your girl is a whore.'

Because they were friends I cursed them out and kept it moving. And what they said may have been true but it meant nothing to me. I knew her as they didn't. And I saw Alicia every day until she graduated. We eventually moved in together and I would grow jealous anytime a man would talk to her and she had such an affable personality that there wasn't a man on campus that didn't talk to her. They loved her. The ladies on the other hand. Well that was a different story.

What I found was that my Alicia would do just about anything for you. And when it came to men that may have included sex but she wasn't unlike any of the rest of us in her desire to be loved and in the three years I was with her on the campus of California State University I can honestly say without any apprehension that she never cheated on me and was as good a woman as I've had before or since then. But for Alicia things didn't always go so well.

Graduating a semester before me she was feeling herself and made it plain to me that she had no intention of going back there again. I begged her to come see me but the world was her oyster at the time and though I have yet to return in the thirty or so years after graduating I couldn't see it at the time. I was there and that in itself I thought was enough reason for her to come back. But she never did and I grew angry. The phone calls grew more and more infrequent and I looked at myself as nothing more than a toy to be played with. I began to doubt her sincerity and wondered how you could profess your undying love and devotion but refuse to stay in touch. So, after months of pleading with her to just come and visit me with no response I decided it was time to move on. A couple of months later I graduated and called to tell her I was leaving and ask her if she would come and take me to the airport which wasn't very far from her home. Again she declined and feeling betrayed I cursed and cut her off the final time.

I was now back in Jersey residing with my parents when she called me to tell me she was coming to spend the weekend in New York. I had little to say by this time still feeling as though the first time things seemed to be improving in her life and the world was her oyster now that she had a degree she could say fuck me and I held that sense of abandonment deep inside me. I was angry and I was bitter. So, when she called to tell me she would be there the following day I felt nothing. Aside from that she was good for making commitments and not showing up. I therefore, continued on with my daily ritual of going into the city everyday to work and then coming home, spending time with the family and then whoever the hottest new chick was on the phone 'til the wee hours of the morning. It wasn't much of a life but it served me well under the circumstances. I was biding my time until the fall semester when I would begin teaching elementary school in the Bronx. I was even thinking about a relationship at this point and considered my three years in college just a jump off place for the big city where the women were not only plentiful but beautiful. Alicia's dismissal meant little now and I rationalized it by saying it was just a time in a space.

In actuality, I was crushed but refused to look back as the future loomed large.

I contemplated going out that Friday night. It was payday and I hadn't been out in who knows how long but after working all week and the two hour commute to Brooklyn every day I hardly had any energy left when it came time to go out. And so after dinner I lay across my bed and dozed off when I heard my mother call down to me.

The house was a split level ranch style and I had the bottom half which was a full apartment in and of itself. Relatively new, it contained two bedrooms a full bath, a living room and a kitchen. My parents remained in the upstairs portion the majority of the time recognizing my need for independence and autonomy.

On this particular Friday, my mother summoned me.

"Tran' there's someone here to see you."

I couldn't imagine who it was but I dressed quickly and headed upstairs. When I got to the top of the stairs I was shocked and had to admit pleasantly surprised to find my old love standing looking just the way I remembered her cute little ass. My parents and she went through the formalities. When that was over we went downstairs where we rehashed our final days. I was still angry at the way things had ended and I suppose it hadn't been all strawberries and cream after graduation for Alicia as she professed her love for me once more. I loved her but felt cheated and abandoned when she left and refused to return to come visit or see me. I wondered how she could fly to New York but couldn't see fit to make the forty five minute drive to come see me at school and I wondered what kind of love this was. Before the night was over she made love to me in an attempt to show me that she still cared and loved me but I thought of all those days and night I lay there thinking, wishing, hoping, praying that this woman that I loved so very much and who professed her love for me refused to come and see me during my final days in college.

So, when she asked me to come and spend the weekend with her at her hotel in New York I refused and watched as she got on the bus alone to make the trip back to New York.

My anger hadn't subsided a year later when she proposed to come to New York again to see me. I was living with a woman in Queens now and after inquiring as to my whereabouts called back to say that she was staying at the Bristol Hotel not far from the house.

I missed her dearly by this time but still angry and calloused managed not to give in and refused to go see her. I still kept in touch with her mother concerning her whereabouts and checking to see if she was okay and was told that she was fine and had relocated to D.C. where she was doing quite well. She also stayed in contact with my younger sister who was now living in D.C.

A few years later, I drove my mother to D.C. to see my sister who informed Alicia. Married now it hardly seemed to matter. She asked me out and my mother and sister insisted that I go. I saw no future and only trouble being with this married woman but after the insistence of all I conceded to go.

Now I'm not sure if I mentioned this before but one of the qualities I liked in Alicia was the fact that she wasn't all there. It is not something that can be taken lightly or dismissed easily if you are to understand her. She is and has always been two shades to the wind or for better more common terminology all the bricks aren't in the wagon.

This was never more evident than when she proposed that I go with her to her house where she resided with her husband. I went with much reluctance and trepidation after her assurance that he wasn't home and wouldn't be but after glancing around the exquisitely decorated apartment it was only to obvious that this man had invested a considerable sum in their home and I'm sure he'd invested in his wife too. So after a quick glance and a kiss I pleaded with her to leave. Her intentions were obvious and I refused her advances again insisted on our leaving. The only thing I could envision was a jealous husband in his rage killing her and then me.

We left but it was plain to see what her objective was and from there we proceeded to another place of residence. This time she told me it was her uncle's house. To this day if I were put on a polygraph I could not honestly say that I believed her. Alicia has always had a way with men. Whether it be that she comes across as truthful and innocent and upstanding or whether it be her sexual prowess in bed she can make a man think he's thirsty in the ocean and sell sand in a desert. She has that knack. I knew deep down inside that some man had given her the key to his apartment knowing her and trusting her to be loyal to him and only him. If he had walked in during the hour or so we spent he would have known differently.

"We always made good love," she said to a still somewhat reluctant me about being with this woman who had already broken my heart. What is it they say? The first time things go astray its shame on you but if I allow you to abuse me again its shame on me. And here I was about to let her get next to me again.

We had sex and it was the same as it had always been. She liked it rough and I took out all my hurt, anger, trepidations and anxiety on and in her. When we left she smiled broadly. She'd been fulfilled, her dream realized. Among the many thoughts I had when it came to this woman was that in a way she had a love/hate relationship when it came to men. She loved men but only as far as she could use and manipulate them. After the hurt at the hands of men she no longer looked at them as innocent creatures but merely saw them as potential victims. Now the only question to her was she going to be a victim or victimize them. She chose the latter and there were no passes.

The fellow that she finally ended up marrying was he himself a victim showering her with gifts and love. No longer able to respond to true feelings of love she took what he had to give then cheated on him with four or five others but whether one believes in the teachings of Jesus Christ or fate or the inevitable karma one thing is for sure. What goes around comes around. And so it was with

Alicia B who by this time had given up chasing the idea of catching lightning bugs, and yellow butterflies that always flirted slightly out of her reach. There were no more dreams of catching yellow butterflies or men that resembled daddy or marriages that resembled her parents. Those dreams had long ago flown away or existed just slightly out of her reach. She had no more time for dreaming and the more she cheated on this man that loved her the further she moved away from her center, her roots, and where she had come from. She was in D.C. now where there were more men than a little bit. It was like a rat in a cheese packing factory and the ability to date three or four at a time was nothing to her.

Funny thing though and I'm not sure if it was out of pure guilt or just the fact that she couldn't stomach the idea of being married to such a weak man. To her there was no challenge. He simply couldn't get it done for her. She did as she pleased and took advantage of his kindness at every turn. My God how that man loved her but she had been through the wringer. She no longer looked for Mr. Right but Mr. Right Now and if came to her he better come correct. Whoever said that the ratio was eight to one women to men in the D.C. area hadn't met Alicia B. who had more than her share and then some. Still there remained something of Hattye and Ernest's teachings when it came to right and wrong and so when she paused just long enough to think of her husband she broke down and asked for a divorce.

Rid of her ball and chain Alicia continued to date, watching men, aware of their games and playing the game at full tilt now. Beat them before they beat you became her new mantra and though love had all but disappeared from the picture she continued her pursuit. Long gone was the idea of meeting her knight in shining armor and living happily after. But still she yearned for a decent man. A man who was at least sincere...

There was the young boy Bryant. He was one of the reasons for her divorce. She'd met him at The Club, a pretty prominent club in the heart of D.C. owned and run by D.C.'s Black police officers. She'd dated him for over a year and they'd hit it off pretty well. Alicia didn't know what his obsession was with her but if nothing else he seemed sincere and God knows he was persistent. Still, always one to try and with the recent separation from her husband she conceded after his constant prompting that she move in with him. She liked him too despite the age difference but in the end he was no different than all the others with women calling at all hours of the night. There was no reason to get upset anymore and though she hoped with each new relationship it would be better she had long since concluded that they were all the same and cheating came as natural to men as brushing their teeth. But why? Why did they invite her in to disrespect her? Why couldn't they just be satisfied with having one woman, loyal and devoted? She wondered if simply by her nature she were too good to them. It wasn't long before the relationship had run its course like all the others and she was in her own apartment.

Alicia's love hate relationship with men was soon back on track. The fact that she loved her Black brothers more than life itself refused to let her pump her brakes and prompted her to jump right back in the fray and a few weeks later she found herself back in The Club.

"Anthony," the young handsome Black man said sticking his hand out. Alicia ignored it. On any other night she would have welcomed the company but she was still trying to clear the cobwebs of another relationship gone awry.

"So, you're not in the mood? Rough day? I can sympathize with you. You should be in my line of work?"

He had her attention now. Alicia wanted someone to talk to but she couldn't call Kim or Sharon. They'd told her before going in that Bryant was too young and was still out there sowing his oats but he'd begged and pleaded for the chance and with her being estranged from her husband and residing in the house it made it difficult to coexist. And if there were any truth in his sincerity Bryant seemed the logical choice and the easy way out and if it made any difference Bryant had a little bit of thug in him that always kept thing a little dangerous and exciting and she had to admit she liked that. The one thing she didn't expect and the farthest thing from her mind was falling in love. Those days were over and hardly seemed possible anymore. She was thirty two now and had been through the fire. Bryant was a baby at twenty five but subconsciously there was that need. There had always been that need for a man to lock her up within his love and make her his queen and sole possession devoted to her and only her. But this young boy hardly met her standards. And still she fell in love. She had to admit he had a certain easy going charm, a certain gene-se-qua and she was soon addicted but he was too young and that same charm she became so enamored with kept other women enticed as well and they called with indignity.

"Hello. Is Bryant there?"

"Who is this?"

"The woman he's sleeping with."

"I guess that makes two of us. I'm the one living with him and sleeping with. So what does that make you? Just another one of his ho's he's picked up on the street? Don't get it twisted and get your hopes up honey. You're nothing special and not the only one that calls here. You're just one of many," Alicia said coolly before hanging up the phone. She hadn't lied but she was tired of the phone calls, the other women and thought of the commercial about sexually transmitted diseases. All she had to do was multiply the women exponentially and if she knew little else she knew she was a prime candidate for some sexually transmitted disease and AIDS. Bryant did little to hide his philandering which left her little choice but to leave but not until falling in love with him as well. They hadn't been together that long but it hadn't made the pain any less. Bottom line was she'd failed again and Alicia was soon coming to the realization that no matter what she did perhaps relationships just weren't meant for her. But there was always some new guy with the same old line about how he was different when in reality they were all the same.

"So, you're not going to tell the nice, gentleman who just bought you a drink your name?"

Alicia snapped back from her daydreaming and saw the double of Patron in front of her.

"Thank you but you shouldn't have."

"Thought it a cheap price to pay for a name," Anthony said politely. She had no idea who he was but he certainly commanded a certain degree in the club. So much so that Alicia was forced to take a second look.

"The name's Alicia short for Allison."

"Nice to meet you Allison. I was trying to wait you out. You seemed to be in deep thought," he said smiling.

"I guess I was. I just went through a rather tumultuous beak up and I guess I'm not quite over it yet."

"Those can be rough. Just lost someone myself not too long ago."

"You over it?"

"Don't know that I'll ever get over it. My wife of twenty four years succumbed to cancer about two months ago."

"Oh, I'm sorry," Alicia said feigning compassion. "That cancer is a bad boy."

"Yes, it is but at least I know she's out of pain and in a better place," he said the pain visible on his face.

A young Hispanic waiter stood, waiting patiently by his side.

"Yes sir."

"Mr. Sims the couple at the second table said that you were going to comp their drinks for some reason or another. I'm not exactly sure why although the gentleman explained it to me."

Looking over and recognizing the couple, Anthony waved.

"That's my boss, Captain Windstrom. Make sure he's well taken care of Angel. I hear he tips well," Anthony said still smiling and signing off on the receipt Angel had given him.

"No problem Mr. Sims."

"Sorry for the interruption Allison. It's always something."

"You're working. Are you the manager?"

"Something like that. Actually Alicia I'm moonlighting. A few of my buddies who I worked with on my 9-5 opened The Club about a year and a half ago. So, I guess that would make me part owner. We take turns working it."

"And the gentleman over there in uniform is your boss?"

"You mean Captain Windstrom? Yes, he's my boss on my other job."

"And what would that be?"

"I'm a sergeant on the D.C. police department."

"That's interesting. So, this place is owned and operated by D.C. cops?"

"I prefer public servants or police officers."

"I'm sorry. No slight intended," Alicia smiled sheepishly.

She had never been a fan of the police but Anthony seemed nice enough. Maybe he was different. He was certainly handsome enough but then how many handsome men had she come across that turned out to be downright ugly after getting to know them? But he seemed nice enough to chat with and she owed him that after all he'd been nice enough to buy her a drink.

Two hours later she was still sitting there enjoying every minute of Officer Anthony Sims. Two years later she was as much in love with him as that very first night. Finally Alicia she thought as she arrived home showered and prepared to fix dinner. Following dinner she would put that cute little blue dress on Ant liked so much and head over to The Club for a night cap. Meeting him after his shift had become a ritual by this time and one she enjoyed. All those beautiful people and he only had eyes for her. It was such a relief to have Alicia found that special someone. Finally! Mr. Right.

Arriving at The Club at ten forty five she ordered a Hennessey over ice and felt the warmth flow through her body. She would have one more when he arrived but no more than that. They'd go home and make love after that and she didn't want the alcohol to take away from the joy of making love to her man. Alicia smiled. It was the first time since she was a little girl and daddy used to pick her up then throw her up in the air and catch her on the way down could she remember being this happy. No longer did she think about that elusive yellow butterfly just out of her reach that she had lunged grasping for only to see it light on the daffodil a foot away. No, after who knows how many men she had Alicia found that one man, her soul mate, her Mr. Right. They'd met in their grief, leaned on each other and arisen from the ashes like a Phoenix rejuvenated and bon again with renewed faith in life and love and possibilities.

Sipping the last of the Hennessey, Alicia glanced at her watch. Eleven fifteen. She glanced around. This was unusual. Anthony prided himself on being prompt. This was so unlike him.

Angel reached across the bar.

"Telephone Ms. Bell."

"Hello," Alicia answered half expecting to hear Anthony's voice on the other end but it was not Anthony's voice that greeted her.

"Yes, Ms. Bell. This is Captain Windstrom. I don't know if you remember me but we've had the pleasure of meeting on several occasions."

"Yes sir. I remember you."

"Ms. Bell I wish I could say I was calling you under better circumstances. I'm so sorry to inform you that Anthony was killed during a routine sobriety check by a drunken driver."

Alicia sat back. Numb she wondered if she were dreaming. If it were all just a bad dream but as fellow officers and friends approached wishing their deepest felt condolences with tears in their eyes the reality set in. After a half an hour she'd gathered herself to let someone drive her home although for the life of her she couldn't recall who it had been. How many hours had she been sitting in that same place on the same loveseat in front of the same television while it spoke of the best insurance and what dishwashing liquid cut grease and grime. It was all a blur to her. She was in shock and remembered little aside from Sharon stopping by and putting her to bed before digging through her purse and shoving a Valium down her throat.

In the two years since Anthony's passing Alicia had a chance to sit back and reflect on her life. What she saw she didn't like but with Anthony she regained the little hope she had in men and the possibility of happiness. The trauma of his untimely death made her stop and give pause. It was true that life was a blessing and the days were not promised to anyone. His death and the direction of her own life forced her to ask Jehovah t give her guidance and during the months that followed she slowly began to move forward accepting Him and giving way to His will.

"What's up girl?"

"Ain't nothing."

"If it ain't nothing why haven't I heard from you?"

"Just been busy. Between work and school it doesn't leave much time for anything else. It's been crazy. By the time I get home from school it's somewhere around 8:30 or 9 and the only thing I have time for is grabbing something to eat and laying it down."

"I hear you. How you doing otherwise?"

"I'm good."

"You sure?"

"Really. I am. I mean I have my days when everything that happened the last few days we were together flashes before my eyes and I break down but overall I'm okay."

"I understand. I was the same way when Dre passed away but you know what they say. Time heals all wounds."

"That's what they say."

"But you know everyone's talking. The girls miss you. And we all think that you'd better off if you would get back out there."

"Is that right?"

"Just saying 'Licia... If you got out there and enjoyed yourself you might not dwell on the past so much. That was God's work. And ain't no undoing the Lord's work."

"I hear you."

"So, you'll go out with us tomorrow night?"

"Let me see how things go tomorrow. I'll give you a call."

"I'll be looking to hear from you. Love you 'Licia."

"Love you more..."

Licia sat back on the bed her knees pulled up to her chin. Kim had been her girl since she arrived in D.C. close to eight years ago and though they were as different as night and day they loved each other dearly sharing each other's joys and pains. But in the time since Anthony's death she had had time to think and she just wasn't there anymore. No longer did she yearn to hit the clubs to see what men she could beat at their own game. And it really hadn't come as the result of Anthony's death. Anthony in just being an overall good guy had helped her regain her faith in men. No longer did she feel the need to go hunting for prey.

'Licia knew Kim was worried about her but what Kim didn't understand was that not only had Alicia's sights changed but her attitude and disposition as well when it came to men. If it were meant to be then it would be but she would not try to force or control it. Her fate was now in Jehovah's hands. He would now be the one to guide her. And there was so much more to life now than trying to corral a man. Still, it couldn't hurt to hang out with the girl's for old times' sake.

"You ready?"

"Where are you?"

"Pulling into the complex."

"Okay. I'm on my way down."

It had taken months for Kim and Sharon could persuade Alicia to leave the quaint, little, one bedroom apartment. But convince her they did and on the night they did it was a sort of coming out party for D.C. and every local talent was in attendance. Still, Alicia feigned indifference. Her thoughts were clouded with Anthony's memory and though she was all but over grieving his loss just being in the club awoke thoughts she had long ago put on the backburner. But in every crowd there's always that one persistent, annoying, guy that just won't take no for answer. His name was Kenny and after a dance or two he was smitten.

Two weeks later he moved in. A month or so later he was a fixture although she could understand why. He couldn't keep a job but the talk of marriage gave her hope that he might just be the answer to her prayers. Years passed and Alicia knew that she was close now than she'd ever been. She could honestly say she was in love. She asked no questions and supported him in every way she could. Sure she was no longer as financially stable as she was when she was married but she had one thing that she didn't have in her previous marriage. She had love and with that as the foundation she could endure anything and everything. Or so she thought until that night when the phone rang.

"Ally, it's me Craig," Ally knew Craig as one of Kenny's boys. He was street and a bad seed and had warned Kenny on more than one occasion that Craig was nothing but trouble but they'd grown up together on the streets of Southeast and for some reason Kenny couldn't seem to cut ties with the riff raff from the old days. It didn't seem o matter that he had a good woman and a baby on the way.

"Ally, the dope boys are holding Kenny hostage on 16th and want two hundred dollars or they're gonna bust him up pretty good. Told me to call you and come pick it up for him."

"I know you're not serious. Do you think I'm just going to give you two hundred dollars? I give you two hundred dollars and chances are I'll never see you again."

"That's fucked up. Me and Kenny have been boys ever since I can remember. I would never do my boy or you like that Ally. Listen. I'll be there in ten so get yourself together. We gotta go get him or those niggas is going to fuck his ass up. I know them niggas and they'll fuck him up Ally. Be ready."

Alicia stood outside the old apartment building and just kept wondering why it was so easy for some folks and always so hard for her.

They were struggling. They were always struggling and now this. So, Kenny was on drugs. On crack… No wonder things never would come together. While she was out there struggling to make ends meet and when they fell short she was always the one that had to pick them up and pull things together. It all made sense now. Despite her working two jobs they were always just one step ahead of the bill collectors who constantly harassed her with their annoying phone calls. Everything was in her name and while he walked around without a care in the world he was spending freely buying this and that and whatever else came to mind. It all made sense now.

She was ready to tell Craig to pull over and let her out. Let the asshole she called her man dig his ass out of this mess. He stayed in trouble; always one step ahead of jail. And she was doing nothing to help him be a man by bailing him of this latest jam. Damn! Still she wanted to hear what he had to say this time.

An hour later, the two were back at the crib.

"Go take a shower Kenny. You stink."

Alicia wasn't exactly sure what to do now. She wanted to curse him out then put him out. She had never wanted children and only as late as last week had considered aborting it but he'd promised to get it together and begged her not to. She'd weakened as she always had but was seriously considering it after this latest escapade. She was convinced that he would never be anymore than a common hood rat like the rest of his family and wondered if she had really been that desperate for a man to have let him into her life.

Emerging from the shower she had to admit he was one fine specimen of a man. Now sitting across from her at the tiny kitchen table he stared at her trying to see where her head was at. Unballing his fist he revealed a small vial of rocks.

"Baby, I never wanted you to know but with you and the baby and this shit tonight I swear this is my last hit. I know that if I love you and want to be a good husband and father for my son I have to change. You're a good woman Ally and I don't even want to consider losing you so I don't have any choice but to quit. And I'm trying baby. I really am. This is the first time in six months that I got high. And I admit it was a mistake. I fucked up. And what I have here is the last time I'm gonna fuck with it but I need your help. I just need to get out of D.C. til I'm clean and strong enough that I can live here. Do you think your father can get me a job in Beaver?"

Alicia was so glad to hear him admit that he was the problem.

"I'll call him in the morning but and if he says yes you can't be going there as my man and be fucking up. It's a small community and everyone in Beaver knows Ernst. It's taken him a lifetime to build his reputation and he's respected by white folks and Blacks so be sure this is something you really want to do."

"I give you my word baby," Kenny said wrapping his arms around Alicia and kissing her deeply, passionately.

Maybe there was some hope. Alicia thought as she heard the lighter flick over and over relocate. She needed after fifteen years to be closer to home. Daddy said he understood and so after fifteen years she was going home.

Two months later, Alicia had saved enough to get a nice enough two bedroom apartment not too far from her parent's home and daddy had gotten Kenny a job as promised. Not too far along in her pregnancy she had no problems finding a job.

Kenny however turned down the job Mr. Bell had gotten him or better yet just not show up and chose to recreate the D.C. thing all over again. Smoking crack, staying out late, and during Alicia to question him about his whereabouts.

And she didn't. Her baby needed a daddy.

It was hard to tell how long this went on but she had to provide a home for herself and the baby. Maybe Kenny would get it together. Alicia thought not seeing any alternatives until returning home from work she set eyes on the large gray and orange U-Haul in her driveway and that bitch Tracy Kenny used to go with carrying the living room furniture she had worked long and hard being loaded into the U-Haul.

"Why you no good lazy ass, cheatin', motherfucker," Alicia said as she grabbed the crowbar from the trunk of her Honda Accord.

Mattie's Confession

Mattie reached over and turned off the clock radio. She wanted to take it and throw it but thought better and swung her thick chocolate legs over the side other full sized bed. There was little space between the bed and the vanity and she wondered if she would do any better than this glorified closet. Well, she certainly wouldn't if she didn't get herself together and get her behind to work.

Walking the five steps to the kitchen she heard the front door slam. Tay had found a little place down in the East Village and Jazz was finishing up her senior year in high school and had already been accepted into Hofstra. The house was so quiet without Tay and soon Jazz would be gone as well. For Mattie it was time to reassess her life. She was paying a little over two thousand dollars a month for the tiny two bedroom hovel they had the nerve to call an apartment.

It was time to make a move. Her kids grown now she neither needed the space or that damn job. When Quadir left right after Jazz was born she was forced to take the first job that she could find to support her kids. The fact that it was as a domestic down on Park Avenue hardly mattered. She could feed her kids but now after twenty one years working for the Hansboroughs it was time to think about Mattie.

Mattie donned the black and white maids' uniform and stepped out into the brisk March winds. She had a little money saved and today she would give Mr. Hansborough her two weeks' notice. Mattie had been giving her two week's notice for close to twenty years now but with Jazz leaving on a full scholarship it was time. She'd already planned on going to D.C. to stay with her sister for a month at which time she'd search for a job and an apartment. But that was jumping the gun. Today she had one item on her agenda and that was to give her two weeks' notice.

"Morning Raul," Mattie said to the Puerto Rican doorman who'd been there nearly as long as she had.

"Morning Ms. Mattie. You're looking quite chipper today," Raul said smiling and holding the door for her. The two had become fast friends over the years and he was constantly telling her that she could do better. "You want to share with me?"

"I will. Let me see how things go first. I don't want to jinx myself. I'll tell you when I get off this evening."

"I'm gonna hold you to that."

"I know you will," Mattie smiled.

Mattie used her key and stepped into the plush Park Avenue apartment at seven fifty five. In twenty one years she had yet to be late and today was no exception.

"Morning Mattie," Mr. Hansborough said not bothering to look in her direction.

"Morning Mr. Hansborough. Will you be in your office this morning?"

"Yes, I will. I'll be there until twelve. Then I have to run downtown. I have a luncheon with some realtors from J.P. Morgan at one. Why do you ask?"

"I was wondering if you could spare a few minutes when you get a chance this morning," Mattie said as she hung up the worn, gray, woolen coat and hat in the hall closet.

Mr. Hansborough paused long enough to check the Windsor knot in his tie.

"Something bothering you Mattie?"

"No. Just some concerns I've been having."

"Is it that son of mine again?" Mr. Hansborough screamed. "Damn him. I'll put his ass out if he's up to his old shit."

Mattie smiled.

"No. No. No. J.J.'s fine Mr. Hansborough. It's nothing like that. In fact everything's fine. We just need to talk is all."

A few years back when their eldest J.J. returned from college he'd been certain he was in love with Mattie. Sincere in his thoughts he'd corner Mattie every chance he got and beg her to marry him. When she declined citing the difference in age and backgrounds he'd pout for a few days only to rebound with a new strategy. He'd even come into her bedroom on occasion after dark with the thoughts of sleeping with her. This occurred until Mattie had a face-to-face with J.J. and Mr. Hansborough but not even that stopped his approaches. It wasn't until a year or so later when he followed Mattie home and some of Tayshawn's boys took him into an alley and had a long talk with boy did he stop harassing Mattie. That had been years ago but Mr. Hansborough hardly knew what went on in his own household.

Mr. Hansborough was a good man even if he had never taken the time for anything other than the business of making money. This is one of the reasons the house always seemed to be in a state of chaos and half-a-heartbeat from World War III on a good day.

Mrs. Hansborough, was the complete opposite of her husband. A traditional southern belle Jody Hansborough was content to sip Mint Juleps all day on the veranda and host supper guests as long as there was a good bottle of gin to help her through the evening. She'd grown out on the island in Wyandanch or somewhere akin and had never been further south than White Plains but she was a traditional southern wife in every sense of the word. I believe they now refer to them as trophy wives. Adept at small talk and the like but if the conversation made its way to politics or the State of the Union Address she was gone with the wind.

Missy, their youngest and only daughter was twenty one and so proper it hurt. Spoiled and brash Mattie had long ago made it a point to avoid the girl and spent a good deal of her employee ducking the blonde monster. By now she'd blossomed from a spoiled brat to a rabid Tea Partier who hated anyone and everyone who wasn't rich, white and didn't have a traceable family crest.

"Mattie did they bring clean laundry back?"

"And good morning to you too Missy."

"Oh, sorry Mattie. Morning. You know daddy insists on giving the business to Lu Chang cause he sold him the building but they never ever have the laundry done on time. Should have left their asses working on the railroads. Damn Chinks! I don't know whoever gave them the laundry business. They advertise one day service and it takes them three. Could you call them for me Mattie?"

"Melissa! I know I didn't hear what I thought I heard. You save those racist remarks for your friends. I won't tolerate that kind of talk in my house. Lu Chang happens o be a friend of mine."

"I wasn't talking about Lu Chang specifically daddy. I was talking about the Chinese in general. And what have they brought to this country. Nothing but restaurants and laundries and they can't even do clothes."

Mr. Hansborough ignored the girl's remarks and headed for his study.

"Mattie would you do me a favor and see if Mrs. Hansborough needs anything and while you're up there see if J.J. has left yet. If he's still here remind him that he has a ten o'clock appointment with Bigelow & Brown to do the closing on the Soho property. When you get finished we can meet around our concerns," he said closing the door to his study grateful to have Mattie has his go between.

At fifty six he had a lot to be thankful for. He'd amassed a small fortune over the last twenty years and rivaled all but the largest realtors in Manhattan. But his home life was in shambles. His wife was for all intents and purposes no more than a nonfunctioning alcoholic who had been in and out of the Betty Ford Clinic more times than he could imagine. And J.J. though quite astute with a business savvy that usurped his own simply did not possess the drive needed to take over the family business. And Missy. Well

Missy was just Missy. Never too bright she adorned the page of every gossip column in all the local tabloids for her asinine antics. Her latest intrigue was as a spokesperson for the Tea Party in much the way Sarah Palin is much to their chagrin. Mr. Hansborough was by far the most level headed in Mattie's eyes but then it was difficult to maintain one's sanity in an insane asylum full of lunatics. And here Mattie found her niche though painstakingly for well over twenty years.

Knocking twice, Mattie took a deep breath and held it before enter Ms. Hansborough's boudoir. She seldom but ever left her sanctuary taking her meals here unless summoned by Mr. Hansborough to entertain guests on occasion.

"What the hell do you want? Did Henry send you up here to see if I'm sleep before he sticks his little pink pecker up in you? Is that it? Or is it my son you're sleeping with this week you little tramp?" she said before taking the latest issue of Harper's Bazaar and tossing it at Mattie's head.

"And good morning to you too Ms. Hansborough," Mattie said before easing back out the door.

"Bring me a cherry martini bitch. Shaken not stirred!" the woman screamed.

Mattie smiled and went to the mobile bar at the end of the hall and poured the woman her morning highball adding triple the vodka. It had become her morning ritual and was the only guarantee that Mattie would have a peaceful day. The triple shot of vodka would assure Mattie that the woman would sleep well into the afternoon. By then Mattie would have her cleaning and chores done and with a stiff pick me up at around three she would be out again. By the time she would awake again Mattie would be long gone.

Checking J.J.'s room she found him to be long gone and the room in impeccable shape. In all honesty J.J. may have been the least of her worries and aside from him being in love with her he presented the least problem of all.

Mattie knocked again.

"Just put it down," Ms. Hansborough screamed. And then knowing it was her last day she smiled and said.

"You want me to call Dr.Reinsdorf and see if I can't have you committed? I mean admitted."

"Why you smart little nigga bitch! You just want me gone so you can inherit my family. I know what you're up to nigga. Henry! Henry!"

Mattie quickly exited the room only to find Henry Hansborough standing at the bottom of the spiral staircase.

"She okay Mattie?" he asked the concern readily apparent.

"I'm not thinking she is. May be time to make that phone call Mr. Hansborough."

"I'm inclined to agree with you but Dr. Reinsdorf is out of the country for the next couple of weeks and I would just hate for her to try and adjust to another doctor."

"I'd hate for another doctor to have to try and adjust to her."

"Mattie. Is that anyway to speak about Ms. Hansborough?"

"Sorry sir," Mattie said out of respect for the man she had come to know so well.

"If you could just keep a close eye on her for the next couple of days I'd really appreciate it Mattie."

How many times had she heard that? A closer eye just meant so many more nigga bitches and no matter how much they paid her they could not pay for the abuse. And Jody Hansborough was a virtual abuse factory.

"Was J.J. in his room?"

"No sir."

"Well that's good. Maybe he's starting to take some initiative."

"If I may sir."

"Go ahead Mattie."

"J.J.'s a good boy. He's bright as a whip too. And whether you know it or not you're his idol. If you just let up on him some and didn't push him so much I think you'd be very surprised at the results."

"You don't say. And what gives you the authority to know so much about my son?"

"I have a son of my own. And growing he didn't have the resources that J.J. had but they're very similar in some regards. Both are bright and inquisitive. You plant the seed and they'll do the rest. My son is Columbia Law School on a four year academic scholarship. All I did was plant the seed and have the ultimate faith in him. That's all you need."

"I'll take that into consideration Mattie. Now what is it that you wanted to talk to me about? You said you had some concerns."

"Yes sir, Mr. Hansborough. I don't know whether you realize it or not but I've been in your employ for going on twenty one years now. Every morning I've gotten up and donned this uniform and ridden the train down here to wait on and serve your family. And in those twenty one years I've never been late for work and have done more than an adequate job," Mattie said pausing to catch her breath and fight back the tears.

"You've been more than adequate. In all honesty you've been superb. Go ahead."

"And in those twenty one years I have never received a raise."

"What? Are you serious? You know I don't handle the domestic affairs. Mrs. Hansborough is responsible for…" he said catching himself as he thought about what it was he was about to say before ending with. "I am so sorry Mattie. I will take care of that pronto," Mr. Hansborough said dropping his head embarrassed with this latest revelation.

"I want you to know I raised two kids on that meager salary and lived in a rat infested hovel for all of those twenty one years. Both of my kids received scholarships to attend college and my daughter will be leaving home in two months. For me it's a second chance at life. It's a chance to start over, to realize some to my dreams, to get out of Harlem, maybe go back to school. So, I wanted to come to you personally and give you my two week notice."

Henry Hansborough leaned back in the captains' chair and stared at Mattie for what seemed like eons when J.J. popped in.

"Well, dad I closed the deal on the Soho properties with two more over in Hackensack. Mr. Leonardi did the appraisal and says the combined value is somewhere in the neighborhood of eleven or twelve million and that's before restoration."

"Wonderful, son. Now would you give me a minute? Mattie and I are in the middle of a very important conversation."

J.J. stood there completely aghast. What could this little Black maid have that was more important than a twelve million dollar deal?

"Mattie I didn't know," was all the older man could say.

"And never once in twenty one yeas did it occur to you to inquire Mr. Hansborough. Y'all walk around here so caught up in your own lives that you don't know that other people exist. For twenty one years I was invisible except to run and fetch this or that. For twenty one years and now today I suddenly become human because the person you're so used to having do the things that you don't want to is resigning."

"Oh hell no. Get the fuck out of here! Dad! What is she saying?" J.J. interrupted.

"I know son. I feel the same way. Mattie's says she's been with us twenty one years and has never received a raise while having to raise two children in rat infested apartment off of what?"

"Two hundred and forty dollars a week," Mattie chimed in. "For twenty one years."

"Oh my God! Dad! Why didn't you give her a raise? And with all the places you own why the hell is she living under those conditions?" J.J. said his sincerity genuine as his eyes welled with tears.

"I didn't know J.J. Your mother was supposed to handle the in-house employees and their salaries."

"You can't be serious. Mattie runs the house. Mommy can't run herself. I know you're not serious," J.J. said accusingly.

"I know son. But I just assumed everything was okay and Mattie never mentioned a thing until today."

"And if you know Mattie then you should know she would never say anything. But did you ever stop to ask father? Something as simple as is everything okay with you Mattie? After all she is an integral part of the household and in any ways the most integral part. She's the one that keeps it running."

"What are you acting as her attorney now? I'm trying to wholly understand the gravity of the situation and resolve it to the best of my ability and here you are making a case against me."

"Offer her back pay and compensation then. Give her that raise and anything else she wants but we're nothing without her father and you know it."

"Thank you J.J. Now if you'll excuse us," he said offering his son the door and closing it behind him.

"The boy's right you know. And I do apologize for letting things go this long without inquiring. You know Rome wasn't built in a day but if you could just give me one day I'd like to see if I can't come up with a proposal a sort of compensation package that will sort of ease all the pain and suffering you endured while in my employ. Just give me 'til tomorrow and we can sit down and talk again. Can you do that for me?"

“I suppose I can Mr. Hansborough. I’ve been doin’ it for twenty one years. I suppose I can do it for one more day.

Mattie held out her hand to shake sealing the deal. But Henry Hansborough wasn’t having any of that at this point. He took her into his arms and hugged her tightly.

“You know J.J.’s right. You are the glue that holds this family together Mattie. So. We’ll meet here at nine a.m. tomorrow morning if that’s good for you?”

“That’s fine sir,” Mattie said smiling inside.

She had no idea what Mr. H had planned for the coming day and didn’t really care. She’d come to the end of the road as far as being the Hansborough’s maid or anyone else’s for that matter so his little compensation package was pretty much a moot point but she always remembered her advice when it came to burning bridges. Besides with this being her only job she would need him for a reference.

The rest of the day went off without a hitch. Even Ms. Hansborough was calmer than usual taking her afternoon nap after having her midday toddy. The news of Mattie’s resignation hit the Hansborough household.

It was a funny thing though in Mattie’s case. She felt more relaxed than she had in years. And the next morning felt even better. She needed the time off, the time to do some of the things she wanted to do. It was time to concentrate on all those wishes deferred.

"Good morning Raul," Mattie said tipping the doorman's hat to the back of his head and giggling like a sixteen year old.

"Wow! I missed you yesterday. You were supposed to tell me the good news," Raul said holding the door for Mattie.

"Jury's still deliberating," she said as the elevator doors closed.

"Morning Miss Mattie."

Mattie was stunned. She couldn't remember the last time Missy had addressed her as miss.

""Daddy has instructed me to tell you to keep your coat on."

"Do you know why?"

"I guess he's taking you somewhere. I don't know. Just following instructions…"

"Well, let me run up and check on your mother before I go."

"Mommy's not here. She and daddy got into it last night and I guess he got tired of her tirades and had her admitted."

"Admitted? But I thought Dr. Reinsdorf was overseas?"

"No. I think daddy hit his breaking point last night. No hospital last night. He had her admitted to Bellevue's Psychiatric Ward for long term stay. I don't think you'll have to worry about her for awhile."

"I was never worried about your mother Missy," Mattie said matter-of-factly. "But what transpired to have your father make such a drastic move."

"You know they don't let me in the loop. All I know is I came home and he was on the rampage. I was told to address you as Miss Mattie and to show you some respect or I could get the hell out and seeing how mommy was being shipped out I thought I'd best reel it in and let this play out."

Mattie smiled.

"Morning Mattie."

"Morning Mr. Hansborough."

"I'm guessing Missy told you about Ms. Hansborough."

"Just that she wasn't home."

"Oh, if I know my daughter I'm sure she did her best to fill you in," he said winking at Mattie. "Now if you'll come with me I have something that may interest you."

And with that said Henry Hansborough held the door open like the gentleman he was and led Mattie Greene downstairs and out into the crisp spring Manhattan air to the waiting limo. A few minutes later they were down in the newly renovated Soho district of the city with its quaint boutiques and million dollar hi rises. The limo pulled up and parked in front of Starbucks.

"Two Cappuccinos and an espresso."

Handing Mattie an espresso he escorted Mattie outside and down the block until they reached what appeared to be an abandoned warehouse. Mr., Hans borough rang the doorbell and was surprised when the doors slid open and J.J. greeted them.

"Dad. Ms. Mattie. Please come in."

J.J. led them in to the abandoned warehouse then down the long hall to a manual elevator. The building was old and decrepit and Mattie thought that at any minute the elevator which creaked and groaned would break down. It was soon obvious that she was not the only one having these thoughts as the elevator bumped and continued to moan.

"And you had the city inspectors come in and check everything out son."

"Yes sir and everything looks good. The first and third floors have already been rented out. I'm showing the second two a couple of prospective buyers and the fourth loft—well—who knows?"

"And this elevator?"

J.J. laughed.

"Gives the building personality. But seriously I asked the same thing on my first ride on it and the guys from Otis—you know—the elevator people assured me that all it needed was a lube job."

No sooner than J.J. said that than the elevator lurched to a stop. Mattie grabbed her stomach.

"Welcome to the loft," J.J. said ushering both his father and Mattie in before leading them on an extensive tour.

Mattie had to admit the place was gorgeous. She'd read and viewed pictures of old abandoned warehouses which were now being converted into luxury apartments and selling upwards of millions of dollars depending on their location. In the new trendy Soho district of the city this one could fetch a million easy from the pictures she'd seen in apartment and real estate magazines she browsed. She used to dream of one day owning one just like this but those dreams had long since dissipated. Still it was nice to dream.

"What do you think Mattie?" J.J. asked excitedly. "You think I can get seven hundred and fifty thou- for it?"

"Easily!"

"Do you like it," Mr. Hansborough asked.

"It's gorgeous," she replied wondering why these white folks had dragged her down here to view something she could only dream about. What was it with white folks? Did they have no heart, no compassion? Hadn't she just broken down last night after twenty one years and told them how she had gone unnoticed and was invisible to them only to flaunt the gap between their lifestyle and hers. She was just so tired of their unfeeling, uncaring attitudes. If she hadn't needed this last paycheck she would have left right now.

"Do you like the way it's decorated? I actually did it myself. I thought it would give a taste of home instead of letting the interior decorators do it. Theirs always seems so cold. This has a homier feel to it. Don't you think?"

"I do," Mattie responded smiling amiably. *'What did he want me to say? And why the hell is he so excited over something I will never ever be able to afford. I hope this isn't one of his schemes to ask me to marry him again. I don't care how much money he has. Our world's are just too far apart.'*

J.J. was overjoyed.

'And well he should be.' Mattie thought. The place with all of its fixings and trimmings was right out of Better Homes and Gardens with its ten foot ceilings and skylight and the open floor plan was to die for. She especially liked the kitchen with its stainless steel appliances and pots and pans' hanging down over the island. It was out of this world.

The library intrigued her as well. An avid reader the shelves held a variety of books covering a plethora of topics. There was even a small section of African American literature lending her to believe that the prospective tenants would be Black folks. White folks sure were devious. Some small reference would show just how liberal they were and might just be the thing to sway them. Of course the way J.J. was going on about the place it was obvious this was to be his. He'd decorated the loft to his liking an obvious reward for closing the deal yesterday, his first major coup. It was about time he moved away. He probably had more sense than all the rest of the family combined.

"So, you really like it, Mattie?"

"Yes, J.J. I love it. I'm happy for you. I really am. It's about time you cut the apron strings."

Henry Hansborough who had been sitting on the settee nearby on a conference call placed the tiny cell on the table and approached the two who were chattering away.

"Well, Mattie what do you think?"

"Think of what, Mr. Hansborough?"

"The place."

"It's to die for. I was just telling J.J. that it's high time he cut the apron strings and got out on his own."

“I couldn’t agree more,” he said shooting a part glance at his son. “But we’re not here to talk about J.J. We’re here to talk about you.”

“I’m sorry I don’t understand, Mr. Hansborough.”

Digging into his wallet he handed Mattie a small piece of paper. Opening it slowly Mattie was speechless.

“A little something in the way of back pay or if you’re still inclined to leave us I guess you can call it severance pay. The loft is also yours upon the contingency that you remain in our employ.”

Mattie couldn’t believe it. Looking at the check with all those zeroes at the end she was at a loss for words.

White folks sure were something.

LaToya Jones

LaToya and me had been friends ever since I can remember. We lived side by side in a duplex in an ol' run down. When we was young—I mean kids—we and LaToya used to do everything together. Sometimes we'd just sit on the front porch while grandma and her mom talked and swing on that old porch swing and swing and listen to them talk about everything from the next door neighbors to some old nasty recipes for succotash. Yuck! Neither me nor LaToya liked succotash no matter how many new recipes grandma and Ms. Jones came up with.

I guess we was more like brother and sister than anything else. All I knew was that she was always there. When grandma opened left the screen door open in the springtime LaToya was there. It was kinda like she lived with us. I didn't pay her no mind most of the time. She was just there. She used to get on grandma's nerves though and whereas I knew how to stay out of grandma's hair LaToya just couldn't get it. I wouldn't say she was bad or nothing like that. She was as grandma put it just plain irritating. I don't think she meant to be. She was just different was all. Me, I knew by the time I was four or five how to get around grandma and her moods. If I hadn't I would have felt the belt or the back of her hand. But LaToya just didn't get it. She'd walk in and in five minutes grandma was ready to tear her new one.

I remember us starting kindergarten together. We were in the same class. We used to walk to school and home together every day. By the time we reached first grade things started to change. Our teachers used to have to take extra time to help her LaToya with her A, B, C's. and counting. The other kids in the class would laugh and talk about her and call her names like slow and retard and stuff like that and throw stuff at her on the way home from school. I'd stick up for her and get in fights with them. Then they'd say stuff like she was my girlfriend which made me really mad cause I didn't like girls like that. I didn't care who it was. I didn't like girls. So, I would fight. Sometimes they would try to stuff rocks in her mouth and do other stuff that made me mad. Sometimes for no reason they would just walk up to her and trip her and knock her down. LaToya would try to fight back but she wasn't no fighter. Most of the time she would just break down and start crying. And it would make me feel bad for her. I knew she hadn't done anything 'cept for being LaToya. One day I told grandma about how the kids treated LaToya and she told me I was a good boy for standing up for my friend and that one day I would make a good man. Grandma's approval made me feel good so I kept on standing up for Toya. And then one day I went to school and Toya wasn't there. I didn't see her for the next couple of days and when I asked grandma if she's seen't her she said she hadn't and suggested I go knock on the Jones' door if I was so concerned and that's just what I did.

"Hi. Mr. Jones. Is Toya alright?"

"She's fine Thomas."

"Well, how come she ain't been going to school then?"

"As you probably know, LaToya was having some problems in that school. So, her mother and I decided to take her out."

"Ah you didn't have to do that Mr. Jones. I didn't let them pick on Toya. If they did I'd give them a fat lip and a black eye," I responded.

"I know," Mr. Jones said smiling. "You're a good friend Thomas and we appreciate that but LaToya has some other problems. She's having a hard time keeping up with her schoolwork so we thought it best to put her in another school for children with special needs so she could get help with her problems."

"Sometimes I have problems in math too. My grandma helps me. Now I get it. Maybe I could help Toya with her math too."

"I think her problems go a little deeper than that Thomas. You see when Ms. Jones and I adopted LaToya we knew this day was coming. She has an affliction called autism."

"Does that mean she's retarded like the kids say?"

"No son it doesn't mean she's retarded son. It just means LaToya's brain doesn't function the way yours and mine does. It just means that she's different."

"So, we can't walk to school together anymore?"

"No, Thomas. LaToya we'll be riding the school bus with other children who have similar problems."

"Well, she can still come out and play can't she?"

"I don't see why not. Let me see if she's finished her chores yet Thomas," he said smiling before turning and going to call Toya.

I liked Mr. Jones. He never treated me like a little boy but always spoke to me like he was talking to another grown up and I always liked him for that. I liked him even more as I got older and understood a little more. Seems he and Ms. Jones adopted Toya knowing full well she was artistic or whatever you call it. Anywhere they adopted her knowing she had some problems.

Still and all, those days were great but as I got older I realized that LaToya still remained seven in her thinking and when the rest of us started going to the movies and venturing away from home Toya was content to stick close to home. It was like she was stuck in a time warp or something. She just never grew up. When I got older a lotta kids would just say she was simple and I guess she was sorta simple but she was still my friend.

It was funny but while my friends were running around experimenting with different things and getting into trouble just trying to get some of those good feelings that used to come so easily when we were making mud pies and having snow ball fights. Everything was fun then. Grandma tried to explain it to me. She said with maturity comes a loss of innocence. I don't exactly understand what that means but one thing I do know is that life ain't half as much as fun as when we were younger playing freeze tag and chasin' lightnin' bugs. That I do know. And all the things I thought was so cool about growing up and being an adult and all it's cracked up to be even though I ain't all the way grown up yet. I'm only sixteen. Been sixteen for two months and it ain't everything I thought it was going to be.

All of my friends are older than me—like seventeen or eighteen and they way worse off than me. Like right through here we all looking or tryin' to get a girlfriend for sex and stuff like that. I guess that's what boys like us is supposed to do when we get to be this age but ain't none of us having too much luck even getting' a girl let alone some sex. They say dudes and girls mature at a different rate and I guess this is true 'cause I don't seem like girls is interested in getting' any sex at all. Sometimes I lay awake late at night and my body's on fire I need some so bad and I wonder why God didn't make it so guys and girls matured at the same time so they would want it as bad as we do. Which is why when they say Toya's simple I think to myself that she a whole lot better off than we is 'cause she just as happy sittin' on the front porch listenin' to her MP3 playa and swingin' on the porch swing than she was when we was just kids. Toya ain't got no problems and is just as happy sittin' there swingin' as she was when we was five.

Everything else is pretty much the same though. Grandma's getting' older and don't mess with me half so much anymore. I think we come to a mutual understanding or maybe she just getting' too old to care about what I be doin'. I don't know. Mr. and Ms. Jones still the same though. They still treat me pretty good and even though Toya and I don't go to school together anymore they appreciate the fact that I still look out for Toya and don't let nobody mess with her.

Every now and then she'll be coming from the store or just coming out to sit on the swing and I'll already be out there and she'll approach me.

"Thomas, do you mind if I sit on the swing?"

And I answer her the same way I've been answering her for the last ten years.

"Sure Toya."

"Thank you Thomas. Say Thomas..."

"Yeah Toya."

"Do you like rap music?"

"Yes Toya," My patience is wearing thin 'cause it's the same question every time I see her. Then she's gonna ask me who I like and burst out laughing when I mention someone she knows. But that's Toya. Those are her issues. They call it mentally challenged nowadays but I think she just has a severe case of Alzheimer's. The girl can't remember anything. Anyway, after about fifteen minutes I can't take anymore of her random questioning and usually tell her I have something to do and go inside. She don't mean anything when she asks you the same thing day after day but she doesn't know what she's doing so I don't snap out on her or tell her to shut up like a lot of the other kids but she will try your patience. But, I know it's all part of her disease. Grandma calls it an affliction. I call it a disease but whatever it is she can grate on your last nerve.

Still, I can remember the good times when she and I were eleven or twelve and would go shoveling snow. One time we made eighty dollars and Toya didn't really want any money. I asked her to go and she went and shoveled just because I asked her to. I paid her anyway but that's my friend. I don't even look at her as a girl—never have—she's more like a little sister to me. And sometimes I wonder if something's wrong with me because everyone and I mean everyone still picks at her. They call her names and make jokes about her and if they ever got to know her they'd find out that she's really a sweet girl that's sick is all. Like grandma says she has an affliction. It's weird too ‘cause you never hear of people picking at people because they have the measles or chicken pox and those are diseases too. What I admire about Toya though is the fact that no matter how many bad things people say to her and about her she never has anything bad to say about anyone. I know it hurts her and sometimes she breaks down and cries but she never says a foul word about anyone not even those calling her names. I’m not sure I could do that. I just ain’t built that way. But she does. And whenever you see her she’s smiling despite everything. I’m pretty sure she understands that she’s not normal but she does more with her life than people that are supposed to be normal. She graduated last year and just started culinary school and says that she’s gonna be a chef cause she loves to cook. She gets up at five o’clock every morning. I know because she’s heavy footed and is at the door by six to catch the city bus to school. I’m really proud of her.

Anyway I’m writing this as part of my English assignment. My teacher said we should write about someone we know and respect and I could have written about a lot of people but I chose to write about Toya because she is afflicted and refuses to let her affliction stand in her way. She is truly courageous.

Last week was a holiday but not a federal holiday and so some things were closed and others weren’t. Toya’s school was closed and when I left for school that morning she was out there standing on the front porch with her headphones on. She smiled and waved at me like she always does.

"You going to school, Thomas?" she said that wide grin of hers plastered across her face.

"Yeah."

"I'm off today. We're closed 'cause of the holiday."

"Oh," I responded. "Wished we were closed. What are you gonna do today?"

"I dunno. Listen to some music and wash some clothes I guess."

"Alright then," I said rushing to catch the bus.

"You better hurry Thomas. There's your bus," she said still smiling.

"Yeah. You have a good one Toya," I said running to catch the bus.

Funny thing though when I got to the bus stop there was no one there. I wondered if we might be off for the holiday as well but then grandma would have told me. She kept on top of things like that. Still, none of my friends were there. When I got to school everything seemed normal but none of my boys were there. They must have cut school but they had made no mention of it to me. Of course they knew that I didn't cut school. Sure. They were my friends but they knew that when it came to cutting school, smoking weed and stuff like that they could count me out. They would still let me know what was up though.

But for some reason they had made no mention of cutting today or what they were up to.

When I got home that evening there were police everywhere and Toya and the Jones' were sitting in the living room. Ms. Jones had her head buried in Mr. Jones shoulder and I could see she'd been crying. No one even looked in my direction when I came in.

"What's wrong grandma?" I asked. The last time I walked in and it was like this Uncle Jamie had passed away and although I asked I was sure I didn't want to know.

"Those so-called friends of yours took Toya up the block broke into the back door of that old abandoned house on the corner and gang raped her.

"What?!?!" I screamed. "No! They couldn't have. They wouldn't have."

"Did you see any of them in school today?"

I dropped my head as Ms. Jones burst out in screams and tears as if hearing it for the first time all over again.

"Where's Toya? Is she hurt? I'll kill 'em," I said more grief stricken than anything. "Why? How could they do that? Toya's innocent! She doesn't bother anybody!" I said grabbing my coat off the hook in the hallway.

Mr. Jones got up leaving his wife and grabbed me.

"Thomas I don't want you going out there making a bad situation worse. The police have arrested five of the six so there's nothing you can do."

I felt a little better.

"Where's Toya?"

"She's in the hospital."

"How's she doing?"

"Doctor's expect her to recover. She's undergoing observations right now but she should pull through."

"I want to go see her," I said the tears streaming down my face."

"She wouldn't know you were there. She's heavily sedated. We'll go tomorrow."

I sat there with my head in my hands. All I could think was Toya telling me 'I think I'm going to listen to some music and wash some clothes. Simple pleasures…

Tandy

Tandy first met the three the year before. Well, in fact she'd not met them at all but simply watched from her tiny store front as the three walked along under the watchful eye of their proud mom's eyes on Hollis Ave. on their way to P.S. 34 everyday. They'd been in kindergarten then and each would wave as they passed her storefront each morning and then on their way home each afternoon.

In less than a year they'd all come to be pretty good friends and Tandy had adopted the two little boys and little girl in place of the children she'd never had. It had been a conscience decision at the time but Tandy brought up in a very religious home never met a man that could match up to her own daddy or who she considered a good enough man to be a suitable father for her child. And though she loved men and the thug in them that could make her do somersaults bringing there wasn't a one of them that could lift a candle to her father and so she'd made a conscious decision not to bring children into the fray. Now at fifty five she looked back on those days and mildly regretted her decision. Well, that was up until she'd met Danny, Todd and Bridget with the little girl quickly becoming her favorite. Tandy had quickly come to love them all but it was brown skin little Bridget Gardner who would break free of her mother's hand anytime she would spot Tandy sweeping the sidewalk in front of the little thrift shop and run headlong and jump into Tandy's arms with the biggest smile plastered across her face.

"Miss Tandy. Miss Tandy. My teacher gave me a star today for being a good girl." she would say excitedly. "Danny and Todd didn't get one because they were talking during quiet time."

"You are a good girl, Bridget. And a mighty pretty one too," Tandy replied picking up the five year old. "And Miss Tandy's going to give you something too for being a good girl." Tandy would put the little girl down and go into the back room of the store to the fridge and pull out a goodie for Bridget who would jump up into her favorite chair her two pigtails bobbing up and down. Today it was banana popsicles. Bridget adored these.

"What do you say?"

"Thank you Miss Tandy," Tandy smiled at the little girl who seemed all but too preoccupied with the popsicle to do o say anything else but he eyes never left the older women as she puttered around the shop rearranging the display in the window and adjusting the price tags.

"Can I come and stay with you this weekend Miss Tandy?"

"I don't see why not but don't you think you should ask mommy first?"

"Will you ask her for me? Mommy likes you." Tandy smiled.

The bells on the front door jangled to let her know she had customers. Tandy peeked around a clothes rack to see Bridget's mother. Danny and Todd ran to Tandy, the boys grabbing and hugging her while their mothers chattered feverishly.

"I can't believe these crazy, fickle ass Americans. The unemployment rate is the lowest it's been in eight years. He saved the auto industry and Wall Street and eight million more people have free health care than when he came into office," Bridget's mother commented to everyone and no one in particular."

"Not only that he brought the boys home. Ain't no boots on the ground. Ain't no young boys over there gettin' killed and these fools are distancing themselves from him. I expect Republicans to demonize him but not the Democrats. I can't believe they are actually distancing themselves from him."

"They should be embracing him and championing all his accomplishments. But no you get these idiots like Allison Grimes refusing to admit that she even voted for Barack."

"Her dumbass lost the election right there," Danny's mom chimed in.

"Ladies! Ladies!" Tandy said trying to calm the women's now heated discussion.

"Oh, I'm sorry. Hey Miss Tandy."

Bridget's mother Cynthia smiled and grabbed Tandy's hand.

"I apologize Miss Tandy I guess we just got caught up. But you know I worked the polls yesterday and I can't believe the Republicans took this election. What was it? Less than a year ago these very same people were up in arms about these very same folks shutting down the government and here we are rewarding them for putting close to a million Americans out of work."

"And you won't get it. I've been around a whole lot longer than you and there is a whole lot I still don't get. But the fact that we have Obama in the White House is in itself a major achievement. And regardless of the job he does there is always going to be that element that doesn't want to see him there but he has achieved the feat twice and we know what he's accomplished. And that's good enough for me."

"I guess you're right," Cynthia said seeming to accept the older woman's point of view as Tandy slipped away to help a couple in search of something.

"Is there anything I can help you with?"

"Yes ma'am. As a matter-of-fact there is. My boyfriend's looking for a blazer to wear to my parent's fiftieth wedding anniversary dinner. Something conservative in a 38..."

Tandy led them over to the men's section and pulled out a beautiful Jos A Banks charcoal gray blazer.

"You can start with this," Tandy said as Bridget with popsicle juice all over her face and hands begged for Tandy to pick her up. Business was business but Bridget was a priority.

"Cynthia," Tandy called.

"Yes ma'am," Cynthia said before reaching for Bridget.

"No, no, no sweetie." Cynthia said reaching for her daughter but the child refused her mother's attempts to drag her away.

"Here Cynthia. Why don't you wait on this gentleman and let me tend to baby girl's needs," Tandy said ignoring the child's sticky hands and grabbing her in her own arms and taking her into the back room.

"Can I come and stay with you Miss Tandy?"

Tandy smiled at Bridget and looked at the two boys who seemed content sitting at the table rolling the Matchbox car back and forth across the table.

"Bridget, I told you earlier that you can always come and stay with me but you have to ask mommy," Tandy repeated wiping the little girls face and hands as Bridget stared up at her with those big brown eyes.

"Please Miss Tandy."

"No, Bridget. If you want to come then you have to ask your mother."

The tears began to roll down the little girl's face. And though it hurt her Tandy remained firm. Bridget jumped down from the chair and let out a shriek before grabbing her head in obvious pain.

"What's wrong baby?" Tandy screamed.

The girl's mother was there in seconds.

"What's wrong Brig?"

The little girl reached for Tandy ignoring her mother.

"What happened?" Cynthia said staring at the older woman looking for answers.

"I don't know. She jumped out of the chair grabbed her head and screamed. What is that about?"

"I'm not sure. She's being doing a lot of that lately. I made her a doctor's appointment for tomorrow."

"That's good. She seems to be in a lot of pains."

"I just pray. I was talking to my mom about it and she said I used to suffer from migraines as a little girl. I'm just praying Brig is going through that. My mom used to hang black sheets at the windows. They were excruciating."

"Mommy can I stay with Miss Tandy?' the little girl asked.

"I don't know. Did you ask Miss Tandy. She may have other plans."

"You know she's always welcome to stay with me."

Bridget smiled broadly wiping away the tears.

"Okay. Let me run home and grab her some clothes for tomorrow. Oh and here's the money for the jacket. The guy wasn't really sold on it but his girlfriend and I forced in on him," Cynthia said handing Tandy a twenty dollar bill. "I hope that's enough. I couldn't find a price tag."

"More than enough. I wouldn't have charged her more than ten."

"Did I overcharge her?"

"No. You did fine. Sometimes I think that I'm too cheap."

"That's why you always have customers," Cynthia smiled before kissing the child on the cheek. "Mommy'll be back. You be a good girl Brig."

"I'm a good girl mommy."

"I know you are," Cynthia said kissing her daughter once more before making her leave.

The little girl shadowed Tandy the rest of the night and as usual was a hit among the customers as she greeted each with Tandy's trademark greeting.

"Hi there. Welcome to Tandy's Treasures. May I help you?"

Tandy smiled each time a customer entered. Somewhere in the back of her mind she wondered if the little girl's screaming episode was just a ploy by the little girl to stay with her that evening. Later that night when she'd read Tandy her favorite bedtime story and Bridget had fallen asleep she realized that it hadn't been a ploy at all as the child screamed out repeatedly in her sleep. It was too late to call Cynthia but it her every time she heard the little scream out.

Tomorrow couldn't come quick enough for Tandy. Despite growing up with six brothers and sisters and having to care for all of them at one time or another the little girl's screams unnerved her. Tandy had never heard anything like them and the sharp piercing screams reminded her more of screams of terror than of pain. And the thought suddenly occurred to her that perhaps her baby was being abused. But when she gave her a bath there were no signs of abuse. But then the little girl cried when it appeared that she had to go home. Tandy quickly erased these thoughts from her head. Cynthia loved her only child as much as it was possible to love a child. Still, she did date and with these degenerate men out there these days who knows.

Bridget's periodic scream continued throughout the night and each time Tandy entered the tiny bedroom she found the girl clutching her head in obvious pain. No this was truly not a case of abuse. There was something physically wrong with her baby.

Morning couldn't come soon enough.

"Morning Miss Tandy," Cynthia said smiling and letting the wooden screen door slam behind her. Bridget's face illuminated at the mere sight of her mother and the little girl scooted down from the chair and ran over to her mother before jumping into her arms.

"Mommy," Bridget yelled before wincing and screaming that same blood curdling shriek Tandy had heard all night.

Cynthia looked at Tandy as if the older woman could supply her the answers.

"It's been like that all night. She was doing it in her sleep. It got so bad that I just pulled up a chair and sat next to her bed and tied to comfort her. But she woke up in good spirits. Well, up until now."

"You should have called me."

"Didn't make sense for both of us to be up and worrying," Tandy set putting the breakfast dishes in the sink.

"What should I do Tandy? She has a doctor's appointment at 11."

"I'd take her to the ER now. That baby is obviously suffering some excruciating pain and the sooner they can make it stop the easier it'll be on her. I'd run her up to St. Lukes. I know Harlem Hospital is closer but St. Lukes is a better facility. Now go child. My baby's in pain. Soon as I grab a shower I'll meet you there." Tandy hugged Bridget then turned and headed for the bedroom as the screen door slammed.

An hour and a half later Tandy arrived at St. Luke's to find that Bridget had been admitted and was undergoing testing. Here she found Cynthia tearful and distraught.

"How are we doing?" Tandy asked trying her best not to let her own concern show and taking Cynthia's hands in her own.

"They just took her in for testing. Right now she's undergoing a CAT scan. I came out here 'cause I couldn't take it. They've got my baby hooked up to a bunch of wires and she didn't say a word but it's killing me. She asked for you Tandy. I told her you were on your way," the mother said dropping her head and letting the tears drip down her face.

"She's strong. Whatever it is baby girl will pull though alight. She's got too much life and energy to let anything beat her. But what you have to do is be there and be strong for her."

"I'm trying but Lord knows I don't know what I'd do if anything would happen to her.

"I know she does," Tandy said reassuringly patting the young woman's hands in a vain attempt to console the young mother's grief.

"You know Tandy, I loved Bridget's father and he wanted a child so I got pregnant but the last thing I wanted was to be burdened with a child. But she gave my life meaning. Bridget gave me a reason to live when her father and I split up. I mean I was so depressed but I knew I had to keep going for her. And since then she's been nothing but a joy to me. When I'm feeling a little down she always finds a way to put a smile on my face. I swear I don't know what I'd do without her."

"I don't even want to hear you talk like that. Baby girl is going to outlive both of us," Tandy said smiling as Cynthia put her head on Tandy's shoulder and let the tears flow freely.

Moments later a young Indian doctor made his way over to the two women.

"Miss Gardner?"

"Yes, I'm Miss Gardner."

"Miss Gardner I'm Dr. Ali and right now it's a little difficult to get a true diagnosis without some further testing. What I would like to do is to admit her and run a battery of tests over the next couple of days and see if we can't see what's causing Bridget these headaches if that's okay with you. If you agree then please step to the nurses' station and sign the consent forms and we'll get them started with the blood work right away."

Cynthia stood there in a daze unable to utter a word.

"Thank you Doctor Ali," responded Tandy shaking the young doctor's hand and pushing Cynthia toward the nurse's desk.

"I'm going to need you to sign the consent forms so we can find out what's wrong with baby girl and get her fixed up. Come on Cynthia."

Bridget's mother who was by now obviously by the gravity of the situation and must have gone into shock was hardly comprehending. Dr. Ali noticing this asked if Tandy was somehow related.

"I'm the grandmother," Tandy lied.

"Well, in lieu of your daughter's state-of-mind is it possible that you can sign the consent forms so we can begin the tests?"

Tandy shook her head in agreement and moved towards the nurses' station where she began signing the necessary forms.

"I'm going to assign your daughter a room and give her a mild sedative. It's obvious this whole situation has been a bit overwhelming and she sees to be suffering a mild state of shock in lieu of it."

"That'll be fine doctor."

An hour or so later Bridget and Cynthia had both been admitted and shared a room on St. Luke's pediatric wing. Running down to the cafeteria Tandy bought herself a fruit cup and stopping by the gift shop which doubled as a newsstand picked up a coloring book and some crayons, an Ebony, Essence and a copy of "O" Oprah's magazine and made herself as comfortable as one could make themselves in the Lysol smelling sterile environment of the hospital room.

"Miss Tandy," Bridget said waking up from her nap. "Where are we?"

"We're in the hospital sweetheart."

"Why are we in the hospital Miss Tandy?"

"We're here to see why my little girl keeps getting these headaches?"

"But I don't have a headache now so can we go to your house?"

"Well, we can go just as soon as the doctor says everything's okay with you we can leave and go to my house if that's what you'd like."

"Is mommy getting checked out too?" The little girl asked sitting up in the bed and looking over at her mother.

"No, mommy's just tired so they gave her a bed to rest in."

"How long are we going to be here Miss Tandy?"

"I don't know Bridget but it shouldn't be more than a day or two."

"That long?"

"I don't know. But here I brought you this," Tandy said handing the girl the bag from the gift shop.

Seeing the crayons and coloring book with Dora the Explorer on the front the little girl's face lit up.

"What do you say?"

"I love you," she said not thinking and distracted by the gifts.

"I love you too Bridget but what do you say when someone gives you something?"

"Oh, thank you Miss Tandy."

"You're quite welcome my princess."

"You going to color with me Miss Tandy?"

"If you like," Tandy replied smiling at the little girl.

Tandy closed the copy of Essence and pulled her chair up to the twin bed and leaned over.

"No. No. You get in the bed with me Miss Tandy like when we're at your house," Bridget said excitedly.

Tandy smiled and slid up on the edge of the bed.

"Okay, what page do you want to color?"

"It doesn't matter sweetheart."

"Okay you color this one and I'll color this one okay?"

"That's fine sweetheart."

"My teacher, Miss Calhoun said I'm learning to stay in the lines," Bridget remarked as she made painstaking efforts to stay in the lines.

"Is that right?"

"Yep and she also said that I'm one of her best students and that I'm a good girl."

"You are a good girl Bridget. You're the best and prettiest little girl I know."

"And I never give Miss Calhoun a hard time like Danny and Todd. She always be having to stop. Like right in the middle of a story or during math she gotta stop 'cause they're talking and not paying attention. But I pay attention and don't be interruptin' 'cause I pay attention and try to be a good girl. And you know what else Miss Tandy?"

"What's that sweetheart?"

"When I behave Miss Calhoun will give me and all those children that behave and do the right thing treats. Like most of the time she'll give us fruit 'cause it's healthy and good for us or work pages that are fun to do. Like puzzle and pages to color. And Danny and Todd get mad at me 'cause they don't get anything. I think they want to get special treats but they're boys and boys just have a hard time being good when their mother's aren't around."

"That's very true princess," Tandy smiled.

"Do you think I'm good most of the time Miss Tandy," Bridget said those soft brown eyes now focused on Tandy.

"Yes, I do. But I don't think you're good most of the time," Tandy said watching as the girl's head dropped. "I think you're great all of the time princess."

The glow reappeared instantly on the little girl's face and Cynthia who was now awake beamed with pride at the two's conversation.

"Well, if I'm great like you say Miss Tandy how come Danny and Todd who are bad ain't in the hospital and I am?"

"Hospital's aren't for good or bad people. Hospital's are for those who are sick. It's a place where they go to get well. It has nothing to do with being good or bad. You're not here because you're being punished for something you've done. You're just here because you're sick."

"I'm not sick auntie," the girl said never lifting her eyes from the page and doing her best to stay in the lines.

"Well, let's wait for the doctor to say that. I think he knows a little more about that sort of thing than you or I princess."

"And then we can go to the store?"

"Yes, ma'am. And then we can go to the store. I'm pretty sure your customers miss you," Tandy replied looking appreciatively at the girl.

This was all she had to say to Bridget who took almost as much pride in the store as Tandy. Bridget now finished with her picture with her picture ripped it out of the coloring book and handed it to Tandy.

"For you auntie," she said handing the picture to Tandy who folded it neatly and put it in her pocketbook.

"I'll hang it up in the front window of the store," Tandy said.

Bridget's smile spread widely across her face illuminating the whole room.

"Want me to do a picture for you mommy?"

The tears welled up in her mother's face. Unable to speak she nodded at her daughter who promptly flipped through the pages until she found a picture just right for her mother and with all the earnestness of a young Picasso went about the task of coloring her mother a masterpiece.

"Well, sweetheart Miss Tandy has to go home and take care of some things but I'll be back first thing in the morning to check on my lil' princess. I want you to take care of mommy while I'm gone okay," Tandy said gathering her coat and pocketbooks.

"Ahh, Miss Tandy do you have to go?"

"Yes, dear. Miss Tandy has things to do but mommy's here and I'm pretty sure Danny and Todd are coming by to see you later on today."

"Ahh, yuck. But they're boys. All they want to do is play army and play with trucks. They're no fun."

"You'll be fine," Tandy said extending her arms and hugging the little girl tightly before doing the same to Cynthia.

"You be good princess and I'll bring you something good in the morning."

"Banana popsicles," Bridget said grinning.

"We'll see," Tandy replied.

"I love you auntie."

"I love you too princess," Tandy said pulling the door closed behind her.

Tandy couldn't remember loving anyone quite as much as she loved the little girl and was certainly glad to have her in her life. A child's love was a special, unconditional love requiring nothing more than her being there for her. And whatever void there had been in Tandy's life the little girl filled it with her unbridled zest for life and spontaneity. She was only too thankful for this blessing that Jesus had bestowed on her. Her thoughts were cut short when she thought of the promise she'd made to Bridget. Something special!! Hmm... Tandy stopped at the local grocery and found some heart shaped cupcake muffin tins. She'd make her those heart shaped cupcakes with the different colored sprinkles Bridget was so fond of. Her birthday was next Monday and the early surprise would only make the little girl's hospital stay that much more bearable.

Tandy went about the task at hand as soon as she walked in the door. By ten o'clock her task completed she called Cynthia once more to check on Bridget before laying it down herself.

"She's sound asleep Tandy. Everyone else is worried but not Brig. She's a ball-of-fire chomping at the bit and ready to go. She's been telling me for the last two hours how Miss Tandy is going to bring her something special if she's good," Cynthia laughed. "I'm ready to shoot both of you. Her for talking about it a million times and you for inciting a riot and leaving. You're nothing but a fire starter. I really am starting to believe you two are trying to drive me crazy and then run off into the sunset."

"That's definitely the plan. Get rid of mom and then elope," Tandy laughed. "Well, I'm glad to see you're in better spirits than early. The doctor must have given you some encouraging words."

"Nope. He hasn't said a word. He stopped in before she fell asleep and took her vitals and asked her how she was feeling. She said she was great and would be doing even better in the morning 'cause auntie was going to bring her a special surprise. But no he didn't say anything other than they were still waiting on the results of the tests and they would be monitoring her closely throughout the night. I don't see how she's sleeping though. They're in here what seems like every fifteen minutes just a prodding and poking her but she's sleeping like a newborn. Hasn't uttered a sound."

"Well let's hope that continues. Okay Cynthia you get some rest as well and I'll see you first thing in the morning. Love you both."

"I love you too. And thanks so much for being there for both of us."

"Good night."

The next day was Sunday and Tandy knelt down and said a prayer asking her Lord Jesus Christ to forgive her for not attending church and giving Him the thanks and praise due Him for continuing to bless her and those around her. She then said a special payer for Bridget asking for His grace and mercy when it came to this child who brought so much joy to her life and others as well. Tandy thanked Him for giving Bridget to all those that came into her path and felt her love, energy and spontaneity. She then smiled knowing that he'd heard her then took the cupcakes from the bread box careful not to smash them and wrapped each neatly before covering them and placing them in the shopping bag.

Wrapping her shawl around her she picked up her tiny cell and called ol' man Mark the cab driver.

"Morning Miss Tandy," Mark said before swinging into traffic. "Where we headed this beautiful Sunday morning? To church..."

"Not this morning. Gotta important meeting with a very special young lady up at St. Luke's."

Mark had been driving Tandy to church for close to ten years. Turning around he was surprised to find Tandy staring out into the cold brisk winter air smiling.

"You're not talking my Bridget."

Aware of the man staring and concerned she nodded.

"She okay?" he said unable to mask his alarm.

"Yes, she's fine. She's just in there for some tests. She's been having these excruciating headaches is all. So, her mom and I thought it best we have her checked out just as a precautionary measure."

"Oh! You scared me for a minute. Can't have anything happen to my baby. But I hear you. It's probably nothing. You know I used to have headaches like those. I would literally start screaming and yelling it got to be so bad."

The old man had Tandy's attention now.

"And what was the prognosis? How did you get rid of them?"

"I gotta divorce," the old man laughed. "Headaches went away just like that."

Tandy laughed.

"I don't know why I listen to you. You're nothing but a cantankerous ol' fool."

"True story."

The cab pulled up in front of St. Luke's.

"What do I owe you sir?"

"This one's on me. Just make sure my little girl is okay."

"God bless you and thank you sir," Tandy said smiling before kissing the old man on his cheek.

"If she needs anything don't hesitate to call. You have my number."

"I'll do that. And thanks again Mark."

Tandy walked through the hospital lobby smiling. At five years of age Bridget Gardner had touched more lives in a positive way than most of the adults she knew.

She was still smiling when she got off the elevator on the fifth floor. As alive as the floor had been yesterday it had quite a different feel today. Nevertheless she had nothing to do with that and she found herself fit to be tied when she reached Bridget's room. A nurse met her before she could enter.

"You're Bridget's grandmother aren't you?"

"Yes."

"I think Dr. Ali would like to speak to you ma'am. He's right over here," the thick Black nurse said gabbing Tandy by the arm.

"Dr. Ali I believe you know Bridget's grandmother."

"Ahh, yes ma'am. How are you today?"

"I'm good doctor. Is this about the tests?"

"No ma'am. Would you please follow me?"

In seconds they were in an office not much bigger than Tandy's linen closet.

"Please have a seat."

Tandy sat.

"I'm sorry. I didn't get your last name."

"Brown. It's Ms. Brown."

"Ms. Brown I am sorry to inform you that your granddaughter Bridget passed away last night in her sleep from what appears to be complications from what appears to be an inoperable brain tumor."

Shana's World

At thirty five she had all but thrown the towel in as far as men were concerned. She'd been married once if that's what you wanted to call that fiasco. If she had had half the sense she had now she wouldn't have given him a second thought but she was young and dumb and hungry for a man and before she could get a handle on things she was pregnant. She'd never wanted kids but when she'd gotten pregnant she had little or no choice and both she and Troy had been elated. At the time she really and truly believed that the baby would change him but it wasn't but a month or so after Troy Jr. was born that he was back in the streets again. For the life of her she couldn't figure out what those streets provided that she couldn't provide him. Men adored her--well that was--every man but Troy who treated her like yesterdays old newspaper.

At first she blamed herself. Yeah, maybe she had picked up a pound or two since the baby but when she wasn't working she was in the gym and looked as good if not better than some of those young girls half her age. And still she could not keep a man. Not long after Troy Jr. was born she caught Troy at Infinity draped over some heifer. And it was right then and there that she decided that he would be the last man that would take advantage of her.

Mommy had all but adopted little Troy and she decided to forget men altogether and just concentrate on doing her. Her father suggested she return to school to get her masters and she welcomed that. At least keeping busy with school and work she wouldn't have too much time to think about Troy and the way that had turned out. She still found time to follow him on facebook and his leaving didn't mean the pain went with him. She cried many a night thinking of what a fool she'd been. She'd given her all and yet when it came to men the results were always the same.

Lil Troy was eleven now and though she felt guilty about not spending as much time as a mother should she knew the boy was her parents saving grace. They simply adored him and she wondered if either of them would still be alive if their grandson wasn't a part of their lives. After awhile the guilt subsided some and when her parents insisted that she focus on her life and career and leave Troy where he had two parents that cared about him, loved him and had nothing but time to dote on him she agreed with some hesitation.

Two years later she graduated Magna Cum Laude from the University of Maryland with a master's degree in Business Marketing and soon afterwards left the firm of James and Peterson to go to work for the feds. The growth potential was greater and the perks. Oh my God the perks!! The federal government had access to the world and with the global economy booming she had a chance to travel as she never had before. So, when the opportunity became available she was on it.

Now for the first time since she couldn't remember when, she was working and being compensated for it. Overall life was good. She had a cute little place in Virginia though she hated the hour long commute in to D.C. everyday. She loved her job and over the past twelve years her meteoric rise within the Department of Agriculture had heads turning. She was now commanding well over six figures. It all seemed to be more than any woman could ask for but there was still one thing missing. A man.

The phone rang jarring Olivia from her thoughts. Placing the wine glass down on the coffee table Olivia picked up the phone only to see Kim's face on her phone. She started not to answer but she'd blown her off for the last two days and knew that if she didn't answer soon her girlfriend would go into panic mode and either have the sheriff's deputies shining flashlights through her windows or she'd show up cussing and fussing talking about how'd she'd been so worried.

"Yes love."

"Damn 'Livia I've been trying to get in touch with you for two days now. You back to not taking calls or is it just me you choose not to talk to?"

"It's just you."

"I'll pretend I didn't hear that. I called you I don't know how many times yesterday."

"I know. I was in meetings most of the day. What was the emergency anyway?"

"It wasn't anything serious. Was just feelin' a lil needy and wanted to see if my bff wanted to come out and play."

"It's been hectic right through here Kimmy. Ever since I got the promotion I haven't had a chance to breathe. And you know we just kicked off this project in South Africa. I have less than three months to assemble a top flight team to put this thing together."

"I hear you. It sounds like you're doing big things but let me ask you something seriously."

"I'm listening."

"Do you live to work or work to live?"

Olivia had to smile. Kimmy had never fashioned to work. As long as her bills were paid she was content to live paycheck to paycheck as long as she had enough money to hit the clubs on weekends and inevitably find a husband to take the drudgery of work from her life.

"Unlike you I love my job," Olivia replied.

"That's beautiful but you know what they say. All work and no play..." Olivia cut her off before she could finish.

"That's what you say. I do all the socializing I need to do at work and am tired of going out to these little dives where men don't want to do anything but make wagers on how long it will take to get in your pants. Half of can't write their names and if you meet one that can chances are he's married, creeping and looking for a night affair."

"Ah, come on 'Livia let's be fair. You and I both know there are a lot of bright, beautiful young brothers out there doing big things. And just because you only attract the bottom feeders doesn't mean you can condemn them all."

Olivia knew Kim was right and for the sake of argument agreed. Now she wished she hadn't answered her best friend's call at all.

"How many times have we had this conversation Kimmy? I hear what you're sayin' and I respect your opinion but that's just not where my head is at now."

"Damn 'Liv a few bad experiences and you're ready to throw the towel in."

"Who said I was throwing anything in? That's just not my focus right now. I'm trying to do me. If I position myself right who knows what may happen. If I'm in the right circles and the right brother comes along then hey!

But I'm not going to a sanitation worker's convention to look for a nuclear physicist. If I meet someone in the workplace chances are we're on the same level and share some of the same interests that's a lot better chance of me meeting someone than in those meat markets you go to we're all they do is look at you and wanna know what they're chances are that they'll bed you down before the nights over. I ain't got time for that. I made that mistake more than once and I just ain't gonna keep setting myself up to get my feelings hurt and my ass beat."

"I hear ya but you know my philosophy. You gotta be in it to win it. You can't be standing on the sidelines and think you gonna take home the game ball."

"I don't know what you don't get. I ain't playing no games."

"Okay. Okay. Chill woman. You wanna stay home and turn into an old hag then so be it but let me tell you who I saw last night looking just as fine as he wanted to. I mean this fool looked good enough for me to drop to my knees in the middle of the club."

"Oh hell, that could have been any ol' body for you slut," Olivia laughed.

"I'm just gonna ignore that but seriously guess who I bumped to at the club last night?"

"Go ahead. Tell me before you bust wide open and have a seizure," Olivia laughed.

"Remember that guy who used to chase you around and was calling you relentlessly. What was his name?"

"Andre," Olivia whispered.

"Yeah. That's him. And damn wash he looking good last night. Say, whatever happened to him? You used to talk about him all the time. I was almost sure he was gonna be the one who was gonna scrape the cobwebs off your coochie."

"I gotta go," Olivia replied before swiping her hand against the power button ending the call.

Forgetting all etiquette Olivia grabbed the wine bottle and drank freely from the bottle. Andre or Dre was the last guy she had been involved with and was the straw that broke the camel's back.

Like all of them it had seemed harmless enough. She'd met him on a night out with Kim at Tacoma Station. All in all, it had seemed innocent enough and every time she looked up she caught him staring at her through those big, brown marble eyes and she had to admit he was one fine specimen of a man. Standing nearly six foot two he was neatly attired in a charcoal gray suit, white shirt and gray and black striped tie. His shoes alone cost more than her whole outfit including the matching Michael Kors bag and shoes she was so fond of. Delicious, Olivia thought taking him all in. Moments later he was buying a round of drinks for both she and Kim but there was little doubt that his eyes were fixed on her and her alone. And after several dances she found herself totally taken in by his smooth talk and laid back charm. Hours later she'd rather hesitantly and after much prompting from Kim she'd given in and given him her number never expecting him to actually follow up. But call he did and before long she looked forward to his calls. He called every day at seven and after awhile Olivia found herself rushing home as to not miss his nightly call.

Over time she learned that he was an investment banker for Merill Lynch and a fitness trainer but in the month that followed their initial meeting not once had he mentioned sex or following up on their meeting. Rather he seemed content to just call and listen to her go on and on about her day. She liked that. But in time Olivia began to wonder why he didn't at least ask her out on a date. Nowadays there were so many reasons. He could be married or sexually challenged. You just didn't know but it did seem strange here in D.C. where men would grope and feel and do everything short of try to sex you right there in the club.

But not Dre. No Dre was cool and she figured that as good as he looked and with his job and portfolio he could probably have his pick of the litter so she was sure that's why he was as cautious as any woman. Olivia was cool with the feeling out period but after a month and a half she wasn't even sure what he looked like. One thing she did know was that he like very few outside of Troy stirred something deep inside of her. How many times had she had to cut the conversation short just so she wouldn't say something that would let him know that she was his for the taking then find herself lying in bed wondering, wanting him to take her in his arms.

After a month or so they agreed to meet downtown in Union Station for lunch. Nothing fancy, just a chance to get together. And Lord knows he looked even better than he had the first time she'd seen him but by this time it wasn't his looks that had her. It was his soft-spoken charm and his attentiveness to her every need that endeared him to her so. By the time they parted company she knew little more about him than she did before but if there was one thing she did know and that was that she was going to have him before the week was out.

She must have had a glow about her because more than one of her secretaries commented about her radiance. Even those in her secretarial pool that looked at her with cold steely eyes usually spoke today. And the day seemed to drag on forever. She couldn't wait till he called her tonight but she couldn't wait for that and no sooner had she exited the federal building than she called Kim.

"What's up Kimmy?"

"You tell me lady. You sound like you just hit pay dirt. You number come up?"

"Better than that. I had lunch with Dre."

"Finally. Damn. Where did he take you?"

"Oh, no it wasn't like that. He was taking the train in from Philly so I just met him in Union Station and we grabbed a bite. Kimmy let me tell you. The man is fine. I think I got wet just sitting across from him."

"What are you wearing?"

"Nothing special. I'm rocking this little lavender Jones of New York skirt suit and some black pumps. I had meetings all day so I had to look somewhat conservative you know. Couldn't really rock his world the way I wanted to."

"Okay so what happened? Give me the skinny."

"Nothing really. We just talked--you know--small talk. I figure if he wants to play it coy and close to the vest I can do that too."

"Whoa! Whoa! 'Livia! Here's the thing. Some people can play hard to get. You ain't one of them. When's the last time you even had a date before Dre came a calling? I know it's been over a year."

"What exactly are you trying to imply Kimmy?"

"No, no, no. Don't get me wrong Liv. You are one beautiful sister. Most of these chicks in D.C. would hand over their first born to have your looks. On top of that you're sharp as whip but when it comes to men you're like the Orkin man. You can rid yourself of a man the way he rids a ghetto tenement of roaches."

"Very funny heifer. I see you got jokes today."

"I wish I did. All ahm saying is that after a year long slump I don't think that playing hard to get is not the right tactic for you. How's that been working for you so far?"

"Go to hell Kimmy!"

"All I'm saying is those playing hard to get more often than not don't get got. And especially in D.C. Do you know the ratio of beautiful women to straight, eligible brothers with something going on? It's gotta be something like 20-1."

"I hear you baby girl. That's why I invited him over Saturday night."

"No you didn't! Oooh girl, you must really be feelin' ol' boy. I think the last time you invited a guy over was little Petey Hamill. You remember little Petey Hamill with the runny nose and the cleft lip."

"You're crazy," Olivia laughed.

"I'm serious. You were crazy about him and invited him to your first birthday party in second grade," Kim laughed.

"Oh shut the hell up," Olivia said still laughing as she made her way through the turnstiles at the Metro. "I don't even know why I let you into my world."

"Cause you love me baby and I'm the only one that tells you the truth."

"Listen I gotta go Kimmy. My train's here. I'll call you and let you know how it all turns out."

"You better."

It was Saturday morning her morning to sleep in but not only was she engulfed in the sunlight flooding her bedroom but also with the idea of the day that loomed before her. She had so much to do and so little time. Up until now she'd been selective, picky even weighing the few men she talked to. But Dre was a no brainer and although she wasn't particularly fond of having to pursue a man if there was one man that deserved her pursuits it was Dre. She smiled at the mere thought of him before hitting the floor on the run and heading for the shower. There was so much to do. Showering quickly Olivia threw on her favorite Carolina blue sweat suit grabbed her purse and her car keys and headed for the silver Audi parked across the street from her townhouse. Turning the key the smooth sounds of Kem flooded the car. Easing the car into drive she headed for the beltway when the phone rang.

"Auntie Liv are you still coming?"

Damn. So preoccupied with her own thoughts she had completely forgotten Shana. This was her weekend to pick up Shana. For the past three or four years she'd picked up the nine year old and spent the day with her doing anything the child had a mind to do. It had started as a favor to Kim who was in the midst of an ugly break up from an abusive husband. She'd gone to pick Kim up one Saturday evening when then husband Shane and Kim were in the midst of a heated argument. The little girl stood and watched helplessly while her parents went back and forth. Not thinking it a particularly healthy atmosphere for a five year old Olivia grabbed a few of Shana's belongings and whisked her out of the house until things calmed down. Four months later things had still not calmed down and Shana became a fixture in Olivia's household. Kim's eventual divorce brought Shana back home but not without trepidation from Olivia who still did not view Kim's lifestyle as appropriate for raising a child. So, in an attempt to show her an alternative to Kim's lifestyle. And of course in the interim she had fallen in love with Shana and basically adopted her as her own. Getting off at the next exit Olivia backtracked and sped towards Kim's house when the phone rang again.

"Hey girl," came Kim's voice sounding huskier than usual.

"Rough night huh?"

"I think I had a few too many Supermans."

"The drink or the men."

"Both honey," Kim laughed. "Went to the Half Note in Maryland with Michelle and it was packed like I've never seen it. Faces was playing... you know the all girls band. And I mean they was rockin' the joint. I ain't seen that many good lookin' brothers in one place in a long time. Every time I looked up here comes another one tryin' to buy me a drink and I was cordial so I accepted. Girl! Let me tell you I could barely walk when it was time to go. I don't know what she was doing but around two I bumped into her and she come talking about leaving and going to Charades. I was like the only place I'm going is home and get in my bed."

"And how's that working for you today?"

"It's not. I got a hangover like you wouldn't believe. Feel like Ray Rice punched the hell out of me," she laughed.

"Not funny Kim."

"I know and when Shana came waking me this morning I wanted to tell her where she could go but all she wanted to know was where her sneakers were so she could be ready when you came to pick her up. I was like thank God for 'Livia. She told me she'd already called you and I didn't think anything of it until now."

"Why what's up?"

"Aren't you entertaining tonight?"

"Yeah. And?"

"Well, with you having your first date in over a year I'm thinking that you gonna need all the time you need. You got to get your nails done and your hair did and get the coochie waxed. I know it's like a jungle down there," she said laughing hysterically. "Man gonna think he's on a safari when he hits that bush," Kim said laughing so hard tears ran down her face. "Hold on someone's at the door. Probably them damn Jehovah Witnesses."

Putting the phone down and opening the door Kim stood there in shock.

"No, it ain't the Jehovah Witnesses but Lord knows you need God up in here."

"Auntie Liv," Shana cried running and jumping in Olivia's arms.

"Damn. I don't get that kind of reception and I put food on the table for the little heifer."

"Ahh mommy," Shana whined.

"You ready to go sweetheart? Can't get you out of this den of sin quick enough."

"Yes, I'm ready Aunt Liv. I just have to run upstairs and get my toothbrush."

"No, Shana. You don't need your toothbrush this time. You're not spending the night tonight. Maybe next weekend."

"But why mommy?"

"Because auntie has something important to do this weekend. Now run upstairs and grab your jacket."

The girl dropped her head in obvious disappointment.

"You start that pouting and you won't be going anywhere young lady. I'll keep you right here with me."

"Oh, hell a fate worse than death," Olivia laughed.

"That's what I was calling you for. I was trying to tell you that you didn't have to come pick Shana up. I could have told her you were busy."

"And miss my girl? She's the best female company I have," Olivia said staring straight at Kim and smiling.

"But seriously Liv, you need a night like this where you can let your hair down and just enjoy yourself."

"I can't agree with you more but not at the expense of hurting my little girl," she said grabbing Shana's hand and skipping towards the door. "We should be back no later than six or seven."

What time's your appointment?"

"When I finish with my little girl," Olivia replied.

By six that evening Olivia was worn out. They'd been to Tyson's Corner shopping and then over to the National Harbor just because it was one of the girl's favorite places in the whole wide world according to her.

Running late Olivia didn't have a clue as to where she was going to summon the energy to entertain tonight but when she called to cancel she was surprised to hear that he was five minutes from her place.

Olivia remembered telling him the key was in the mailbox as if it were yesterday. She still had to drop Shana off and with no time to cook she'd stop by Three Brothers and pick up a couple of veal ptarmiagiana dinners and then grab a bottle of wine on the way in. At the most it would take no more than forty five minutes to an hour.

Arriving home little more than an hour later Olivia was surprised to find Dre, remote in hand reclining in the easy chair fast asleep. She smiled and dreamed of the day Dre in the easy chair would become a permanent fixture. For now she would be content to just let him sleep while she showered and prepared dinner.

Hours later Olivia closed her eyes. Dinner was great, the conversation better and the gentleness in which he took her convinced her that this was the only man for her. After months of little more than getting to know one another there was little doubt in her mind that this was truly her soul mate. She felt his firm body against hers as she closed her eyes and drifted off to sleep her mind fixated on having this man, possessing him. The only thing that bothered her about Dre and their budding relationship was that at no time in the six months since she'd known him had he even come close to committing himself to her. They'd, well at least she had, brought up how she felt about commitment and marriage. And though he'd listened he never once uttered a word explaining how he felt. And as she closed her eyes she knew that if she were ever convinced that she wanted to be in a wholly monogamous and committed relationship with anyone it was this man.

The following morning Olivia woke to the sound of birds chirping outside her window and sunlight bathing her. The night had been glorious. She couldn't remember how many times they'd made love but it hadn't been enough. It was glorious and all she could think of was recreating the joy she felt and was mildly surprised to turn and find a note where Dre had been.

'Went out for my morning run. Will scrounge up breakfast on my way back.'

She smiled as she tried to gather her thoughts and pull herself together. The phone rang.

"Hey girl. Is he still there?"

Olivia grinned.

"No. Actually he went out to grab breakfast."

"Breakfast? So, you didn't scare him away. So, how was he? Was he as good as he looks?"

"Better," Olivia said grinning widely now. "Boy had me in tears."

"Damn. You sound like you're all in."

"What's that mean?"

"That means you're half a heartbeat from the "L" word."

"I could very well be. If I were he would certainly be the one. But let me get off this phone. He should be on his way back and I look like I've been through the war. Tell Shana I'll be there no later than twelve."

"The hell with Shana. You stay with that man. Hell, I can't even remember the last time you had a man spend time let alone stay the night."

Olivia laughed.

"Go to hell, Kim."

Tito's Bridge

Fall was beginning to make its presence known and the warm sunshine that used to shower the streets of Spanish Harlem now seemed to constantly be playing peek-a-boo with the clouds when there was any sun to be seen. He hated this time of year. It always meant that winter was right around the corner. And that meant another school year. The only reason he attended was because of mommy but she was starting to get up in age and always looked so tired when she dragged herself home at the end of the day. At seventeen he knew that he was old enough to be providing some assistance and take the weight off of her. He knew it was no picnic working for those rich white folks over on the east side. She was in her mid fifties and had seen better days but Esmerelda loved her boys and made sure that there was always a hot meal on the table for he and Pepi each night.

She hated the idea of him dropping out.

"You're so bright hijo. If you would just apply yourself a little more you can be anything you want to be. Look at the president. He came from a single parent home. But he applied himself. He wanted better. All you have to do is apply yourself and want for more. That's all you have to do papi."

How many times had she told him the same old thing? And as much as he tried he could see no difference. Where Raul and Jesus were hanging out with large bank and the flyest new clothes and talking to all the fine honeys he would drop his head and scamper up the stairs to the fifth floor to the same pot of arroz con pollo everyday of the week.

Sure he knew there was no future in slinging drugs and over time your number came up and the only thing they could look forward to was a lengthy jail record but hey for now they were at least living. But he saw no point, no future despite what mommy said. They were always struggling. Always trying to pay the rent, always trying to put food on the table, always dreaming of the finer things in life. And with everything she and Pepi talked about he could never see them overcoming or getting ahead.

No. A job is what he needed. It would relieve the burden on mommy and allow him to hang out with the fellows without being ashamed of how he looked. With a job he might even be able to hook Pepi up and mommy wouldn't have to work all the time. They might even be able to afford cable. And with that thought Tito informed mommy and Pepi at dinner that he wouldn't be attending his senior year at Lower Manhattan High.

"What mommy?' Tito said exasperated. "You work all the time for the crackers downtown and are always struggling to pay the rent and put food on the table. And me and Pepi look like shit when we go to school. You can't even afford to put clothes on our backs."

Pepi jumped up from the table knocking his glass of kool aid over.

"Don't you disrespect mommy."

"Pepi," his mother yelled.

"I wasn't disrespecting mommy. I was just saying she works all the time and there's nothing to show for it. We've been scraping ever since daddy left. Mommy will tell you that herself. All I'm saying is she needs help. And with me being the oldest it's time I man up and help her out. That's all I'm saying."

Pepi sat back down.

"But what about your education Tito?"

"I'll finish mommy. I promise you that."

"Do you know how many times I've heard that? Your father said the same thing and he never went back. And they tell me it's even harder to make it now without a high school diploma than it was when your father and I were coming up."

"And who's going to hire you with no high school diploma?" Pepi chimed in.

"I already got a job, smartass."

"Watch your mouth hijo," his mother said wagging her finger at him.

"I'm working as a delivery boy at Salazar's bodega downtown."

"Not Luis Salazar! Everyone knows he's one of the biggest drug dealers in Harlem son."

"Why is it that every time an Hispanic becomes successful he's got to be doing something illegal. Why can't he just be a shrewd businessman?"

"Because he's a drug dealer," Pepi said. "That's common knowledge bro. Ask your boys Raul and Jesus where they get their stuff from. They make no bones about it. Salazar bro. Salazar."

"Okay and even if he is what's that got to do with me? I ain't selling no drugs. I'm delivering groceries down on the lower east side."

"How do you know what you'll be delivering?" Pepi asked.

"All I'm asking you to do hijo is to finish this year and then let's look at what's available. If you get a scholarship and go to college mommy won't have to work so hard. That's the right thing to do, hijo."

"And your grades are almost as good as mine bro. You can probably pick your college and once they see your portfolio and your designs you're basically a shoo in to be an architect or engineer. Man you should stay in school."

"I already told Mr. Salazar I'd start tomorrow."

"I bet he didn't object either did he," his mother said disgustedly. "He doesn't give a damn about us. He doesn't care anything about Hispanics. And he had the nerve to want to lead the Puerto Rican Day Parade. I'm so glad the community objected and told him no. He's selling that poison and killing our community, our kids and making them orphans. He doesn't care about us as a people. All he cares about is putting a dollar in his pocket. Do you think he cares about my son and whether he has a future or not?" Ms. Fuentes said as she tossed the dirty dishes in the sink.

"Listen to her bro. You know mommy's telling the truth. She loves you and cares about you bro. You think Salazar does? It's not too late to tell him no bro. Listen you're a senior. In six months you graduate. Then you go to college. You live in the dorm. They pay everything and you get a little job for spending change, buy some fresh gear and hook up with a cute little honey on campus and make some babies. I'm telling you bro, that's the way to go," Pepi said smiling before grabbing and hugging his big brother.

Tito glanced at his mother who seemed despondent now. Locked in some faraway thought, Tito knew her thoughts centered on his dropping out and felt somewhat ashamed for having to add any extra burden on his mother who was already carrying the weight of the world on her shoulders. But damn. At least she didn't have to worry about him being out there in the streets like his boyhood chums who were so deep in the game that there was no way out. Where could Jesus go get a legit job now? Having been arrested fourteen times before the age of age of eighteen for possession and distribution he'd still had a chance. But after dropping out in ninth grade and picking up a couple of more arrests after turning eighteen there was little hope for him now.

Raul was no better. And after a drug deal turned bad some kid not much older than Raul had shot him leaving him with a permanent limp. No. he had never even entertained the idea of selling poison. All he wanted was a little money to keep his family afloat. All he wanted to do was draw and sketch designs for the buildings that he saw in his bed late at night when the lights were out.

Where other boys dreamed of cute chicks Tito saw structures in much the same way the great architect, Frank Lloyd Wright did preferring the low scaled buildings of lower Manhattan than the taller buildings uptown. He especially liked Grand Central Station and wondered why his mother hadn't enrolled him in Arts and Design knowing his passion for drawing and designing. Lower Manhattan had a few arts and drafting classes but nothing like Arts and Design. And despite the fact that he wasn't a student didn't dispel his love for drawing and architecture. Tito excelled in those classes at Lower Manhattan High and constantly received praise from his teachers there. Sure he did well in his other classes but he was in his element when it came time to his sketches. But aside from that school was a drag and he could always go back but for right now he had to make that dough.

Grabbing the dish towel he began drying the dishes mommy had just washed. He too was now lost in thought. He hated to give up his sketchings. It was the only thing he did well and everyone who saw them appreciated and complimented him on them.

Mr. Salazar wasn't at all how Tito expected him to be. Short and gruff he said little and usually barked his commands well that was to everyone except Tito.

"Come here, Tito."

"Yes sir."

"You've been here a little over a month and I've only heard good things about you. They tell me you're good with numbers and you know your way around and you don't steal. That's good. I don't know if you know it or not but this bodega is just one of my businesses. I have some other rather lucrative enterprises that I'm just getting off the ground. You stay sharp and on the right path and you'll go places."

"Yes sir," Tito responded looking into the cold glassy eyes of the short balding middle-aged grocer.

"My son tells me you're taking care of your mom and your younger brother from the money you make here."

"Yes sir. My mother works too but she doesn't make enough to take care of me and my brother let alone pay rent and keep food on the table."

"Well, it's good to see a young man with his head in the right place. So many of our young men think they can take short cuts but there are no such things as short cuts. The jails are full of young Puerto Ricans who tried to take shorts. But there is no substitute for effort and hard work."

Tito couldn't believe his ears and just nodded in agreement. He only wished Pepi and mommy could have heard Mr. Salazar.

Salazar turned to his store manager.

"Luis make sure that Tito here gets a package for his family at the end of each week."

"Thank you Mr. Salazar," Tito mumbled.

"I'm giving you a dollar more an hour. It ain't much but it should help a little. You just keep up the good work." Salazar said before walking away.

The words Mr. Salazar rang loudly in Tito's ears as he swerved in and out of the mid-town traffic. When he first started he had to admit he loved the job. He loved seeing the little Russian ballerina in her studio down on the Lower East Side and the Chinese hustling and bustling at breakneck speed down in Chinatown. His wardrobe was growing but he had no need for it now. There were girls to impress at school but there was no school now. And the few times he thought about going downstairs and just chilling on the stoop and hang out with Jesus and Raul he found that his legs hurt too badly and he was too tired to do anything other than eat, shower and go to bed only to jump up at the crack of dawn and head back downtown for another long, hard day of drudgery. He soon realized that this work thing he had wanted for so long was not all that it was cracked up to be.

Mommy had garnered his utter attention and respect by this time. After all, she'd been making time ever since Tito could remember and she had never whined or complained. She went through her daily ritual getting up at 4 a.m. and often times not getting home until seven thirty or eight o'clock at night.

By now, Tito often thought about quitting but he was too far behind to go back to school now. His pride would never allow him to be laughed at by his classmates because he didn't know what was going on. And he hated the idea of his little brother sitting there saying I told you so.

"Hey man," snapped Tito's head to attention as he set the early morning deliveries in order.

"Hey what's up Kenny?" Tito said smiling at Salazar's oldest son. The Salazar's with all their money lived over top of the tiny bodega and Tito used to wonder why the man known as the Kingpin with all of his money still lived over the tiny bodega. Rich people sure were strange to him and he wondered if he would ever understand how their minds worked.

"Nothin' man."

The two had known each other since elementary school but had lost contact when the Salazar had moved downtown but it was though hadn't passed when they met this time.

"You still drawing?" Kenny asked.

"Here and there."

"Man, you were the best artist in the school. I always wondered what happened to you and what you were going to do with all that talent. I used to tell the fellas that if there was one brother that was gonna make it out it was gonna be you. And I just knew we were gonna hook up again at Arts and Designs."

"Yeah." Tito replied nonchalantly putting the bags of groceries into the baskets on the bike all the time that Mr. Salazar was listening intently to the boy's conversation.

"So, how come you didn't go? With your skills you would have gotten a scholarship for sure and been able to pick the college of your choice."

"I don't know. I guess being the oldest and with my dad leaving I just thought it would be best if I hung around close to home to look after my little brother and my mom."

"Still. They must have some art and design classes for you. Where you planning on going to college?"

"I dropped out this year. Had to get a job and help moms out."

"In your senior year?" Kenny said dumbfounded.

"Don't you think it's time you were on your way?" Mr. Salazar said interrupting his son's questioning.

"I'm just saying..."

"Out Kenny," Mr. Salazar said pushing his son towards the front door. "Unlike you this young man has work to do."

"But papa you don't know. Tito was the best artist in C.E.S. 73X. He could have been the best architect..." he said his voice trailing off as his father pushed him out the door as the cold air blew in the tiny store.

Tito dropped his head and continued to rearrange the bags of groceries as Kenny's words reverberated in his head.

"Pay no attention to that boy of mine, Tito. He's soft in the head. Sometimes I think his mother and I have done him a disservice. We spoiled him. He's not like us and never had to do a hard day's work in his life. He'll grow up to be fat and sit in a big office and push pencils all his life. But you and I come up the hard way and appreciate everything we earn. And I'm telling you I have big things in store for you in my organization so don't you pay him any mind. Now hurry and get those groceries over to Ms. Escovido. You know how she hates to be kept waiting."

Tito pushed the bike out into the cold, wintery air. It was plain Salazar didn't care about him. Tito rode all day around the all but deserted streets of lower Manhattan. It was the first really cold day of the year and New Yorkers scurried like rats to find shelter and warmth. But Tito hardly felt the cold Arctic air that brought tears to his eyes. No. Al Tito could see, hear and feel was the sound of Kenny's voice chiding him for being the best damn artist in the school and dropping out in his last year of high school. The words stung more than the cold air slashing at his face and he knew then that he'd been a fool.

Making his way back to the store after his final delivery Tito was caught in a quandary. He wondered if he should finish working at Salazar's Bodega until the beginning of next semester or tell the ol' man today would be his last day.

Approaching the tiny bodega Tito received his answer. Police were everywhere as a throng of onlookers stood outside the yellow taped off area around the entrance of the store.

"There were three of them. All of them had masks on. They just walked in and started blasting away and then they walked out got in an old green van and just drove away," an eyewitness said matter-of-factly. "Which is okay I s'poze. Everyone knows Salazar was dirty. He's been in the drug game since I was a little girl. He's just like all the rest of them. His number just came up is all."

SHANA

Shana was only sixteen when she had Amir. Jalil was the first boy she'd ever been with and the first boy that had ever really shown an interest in her. Three months after they made it official that they were a couple she'd gotten pregnant and he was with her every step of the way.

When she told her mother, the woman only a few years older than Shana dropped her head. Shana could see her mother's tears but it was too late for tears now. Shana was close to three months pregnant and had agonized about telling momma but now that she was beginning to show she had little choice but to tell her.

"I was one of the brightest girls at Oak Mont High when I got pregnant with you Shana. Was on the honor roll and everything. My teachers had my future planned and had me set up to take the S.A.T.'s and were telling me what college would best suit me when your daddy came along out of the blue. The rest is history and though I never regretted having you I often wonder how far I could have gone."

"I know momma but it's gonna be different with me. Jalil and me are both honor roll students and we both plan on going to college. Plus he loves me."

"I said the same thing about your father baby and I bet you can count the times you've seen your father on one hand and still have fingers left over."

"Ah momma, you don't know Jalil. He's different."

"I sure hope you're right baby girl," Ms. Johnson said hugging her oldest child tightly.

And Shana was right for the most part. That first year Jalil and Shana were virtually inseparable. He accompanied her everywhere she had to go and never missed a pre-natal care appointment.

When Amir was born it was no different with Jalil coming to the house the minute school was out and keeping her abreast of what was going on. Shana had to leave school in May to have the baby but went to summer school a month later to complete her sophomore year and all looked promising for the three.

Jalil got a job that summer with a landscaping company and brought every penny to Shana to help clothe and feed the baby. And when Shana was in school, had an errand to run or just needed some time for herself Jalil gladly took the baby.

"Shana you need to go downtown and apply for welfare. If you're going to attend school this fall you need to apply for child care and food stamps. I ain't keepin' no new born. I've got my hands full with your brothers and sisters," Ms. Johnson said matter-of-factly.

Doing as she was told Shana got up early one morning in early August and was down at the welfare office before the doors opened. A big, black, grisly looking guard looked Shana over.

"Can I help you missy?"

"I'm here to apply for assistance."

"What kind of assistance is you looking for?" he said grinning an ornery, mischievous grin that had other implications. Ignoring the lewd innuendos Shana stared back at the gruff looking older man.

"I'm here to apply for child care and food stamps."

"Damn you ain't much more than a child yo'self," he remarked his grin now transformed into a frown.

Again Shana ignored the grizzled, old guard's attempts at flirtation.

"Sign in, take a number and have a seat missy."

Shana ignored the man's looks, followed his direction and took a seat among the throng of women already in attendance. There were woman of all nationalities, ethnicities, of all ages and all had one thing in common. They all appeared poor. Shana quickly dismissed the thought. Momma had told her earlier that this was no more than a stepping stone; temporary assistance until she finished school and could get on her feet. And that's the way Shana looked at it.

Sitting there Shana buried her head in her book hoping that no one there recognized her. Always at the top of her class she'd always carried her with a kind of reserved arrogance. The other girls used to call her stuck up but she didn't care. Ten years from now when they were still stuck in the projects saddled with four or five kids she'd be in some faraway place with her own office and secretary looking back on just far she'd come. So, let them laugh now. But never, not once did she think she'd be sitting here with the likes of these losers hoping that the government would give her a few dollars and some government cheese to help her feed her child.

Looking around Shana couldn't help but notice a pretty young girl not much older than she was pushing a stroller-you know the ones-that held two little boys no more than two or three old with a third one crying for mommy to pick him up. Shana shook her head in disgust. What was it that momma used to say? The first time it's a mistake but if you continue to make the same error its stupidity.

At seventeen or eighteen with three kids one thing was obvious as the little boy's in the stroller were screaming bloody murder while the third still tugged at his mother's dress in hopes that she would pick him up. This girl, not much older than Shana certainly hadn't learned from her mistakes. Won't be me Shana thought to herself.

Not long afterwards Shana tired of momma's complaining about this and that applied for Section 8 and took the baby and moved two blocks away. It was the first time Shana had a room of her own. Elated and determined to show momma and everyone else that she could make it work she decided to forego school the following semester.

After all, she was young and could always go back to school but right now it was time to concentrate on providing a warm and loving home for her baby and her man. Her next door Ms. Jackson neighbor was an older woman in her sixties who'd recently lost her husband and was only too happy to volunteer to watch the baby when Shana mentioned getting a part time job at the local Dollar Tree.

Two weeks later Jalil moved in and Shana was convinced that life couldn't be any better. She had a man that loved her, a newborn baby that was just as cute as he could be and for the first time in her life she had everything she could have possibly wanted. And with her job and the government's assistance she kept a little money in her pocket. Jalil still had his landscaping job and though he hated it and had dreams for more it would do for now.

One night after the baby was asleep Jalil grabbed and pulled her down to the sofa next to him. Shana kissed him softly.

"Shana, you know how much I love you baby."

Shana who was nestled in Jalil's arms sat up and turned to look at him.

"Where did that come from?"

"I'm just saying baby. Since Amir's been born you've changed."

"And what's that supposed to mean?"

"I mean you've got your own place now and got a little part-time job and you're playing mommy and the good wife..."

"And?"

"And it just seems like you've changed is all."

"How so?"

"Well, when we first met what attracted me to you was you weren't like all the rest of the girls around here. You were different. You had goals and wanted more than what the projects had to offer. All you talked about was where we were going to college. Even after Amir was born you still had your sights set on college but since you got this place I ain't heard you mention college. Now it's like you made it and you satisfied."

"And you're not satisfied?"

"Hell, no. I don't know what tomorrow brings but I know I don't want to be cutting grass the rest of my life for chump change and living in the projects."

"And you don't have to. I'm pretty sure you know where the door is," Shana said her anger getting the best of her.

Jalil stared at her before standing, grabbing his jacket and heading for the door.

Shana was stunned and wondered if she'd told him that she was pregnant again would he have stayed.

The Weight

Aunt Mabel was dead tired. Exhausted…

"Aunt Mabel I can't find my shoe," Tyreke screamed.

"Aunt Mabel can you sign my permission slip so I can go on the field trip. And I need the money too." Malik said.

"Aunt Mabel, Zachary's been in the bathroom forever. I'm going to be late for homeroom and get detention again." Charisse yelled. "Come on Zachary. You're just like a woman. My God I have never seen anyone take as long as you do."

“Gotta keep it fresh for the ladies.”

“Ain’t nobody lookin’at your skinny ass. And Shanice ain’t thinking about you. For your information she goes with Malik.”

“And for your information ain’t nobody interested in no flat chested freshman. I only fly with upper classmen.”

“Whatever! Just get out of the bathroom. You’re making me late again. Aunt Mabel!”

“Lord have mercy! You children are going to be the death of me.” The old woman said pulling the old faded robe closed and tying it as she had every morning since her baby sister had utter misfortune of being sentenced to a fifteen year bid upstate for possession and distribution leaving her five kids to social services. She was the next of kin and had reluctantly accepted the children. What other choice did she have? They were family and she couldn’t just let them be broken up and sent to foster care.

“Where did you take your shoes off? Retrace your steps young man.” She said signing the permission slip and lining up their sandwiches.

“Zachary out of the bathroom now!”

Minutes later the house quiet Mabel put the empty dishes in the sink and smiled. They were a handful at times but she loved as she had her very own. They were good kids for the most part. Sure Charisse was boy crazy but then what thirteen old girl wasn’t. And Zachary was full of himself and since he'd made the varsity basketball team as a sophomore there was little anyone could say to him but he managed to maintain a B average and aside from taking too long in the bathroom he may have been the best of the bunch and her favorite. The twins at nine were still trying to get a handle on life but presented no problems other than being involved in an occasional fight and usually with each other. And then there was the baby, still too young for school who spent her days up under Aunt Mabel refusing to let her out of sight. She could be usually found underfoot or in her aunt's arm.

Mabel sat down in her worn easy chair and drew a deep breath. She remembered the year Chris had gone off to Chapel Hill. A year later she'd retired from the post office and she was finally able to sit back. She remembered Ms. Burney's trips to Atlantic City or the cruises to the Caribbean. Now that was living. How many years had she worked just to enjoy the finer things in life?

And just when things seemed that they couldn't get any better there was that call.

"Mabel Sims."

"Yes."

"My name is Glover. I'm a caseworker with Children Youth and Families here in Allegheny County. I'm calling in regard to your sister Gretta. It seems Gretta has been arrested for the possession, sale and distribution of cocaine. The county has temporary custody of her children and by law we are required to notify the next of kin before placing them in foster care."

"Lord Jesus. You don't know how many times I've spoken to that girl about messing with that stuff. Lord! Lord! Lord! I knew this shit was going to happen. I tried to tell her dumbass. Lord Jesus help those poor children. Where are they now? Allegheny Children's Shelter. Well, that is all but the baby. I have her with a foster parent. Do you think it possible that you or some other relatives would be willing to take them?"

"Well being that there is only my sister and I I guess there's no other choice. Has she been arraigned? Do you know how serious it is? Has she been charged?"

"That I don't know. If you call the Allegheny County Sheriff's Department I'm sure they can tell you more. In the meantime, can I set up a time to come and speak with you and make sure the house meets county specifications to house five children."

"That was five years ago and for the twins and the baby Aunt Mabel was the only mother they'd ever known. She cringed at the thought but had stepped in almost as if it was her calling, her destiny. The baby even referred to her as 'Ma Ma'.

Mabel now in her late sixties had to forego the days of wine and roses and concentrate on raising five younguns. There were no more cruises or two day trips to Atlantic City to wile away the days gambling. Now every extra dime she had went to raising her new family.

"Damn Mabel! You're a good one. Mother Teresa ain't got nothing on you. Shit you didn't even get to have the sex and here you are when the rest of us are trying to enjoy the little time we have left with five kids," Tracy laughed. "You ain't get the feel good part of it. All you got was the results," she said laughing. "All I know is you're a better woman than I am. I couldn't do it. I didn't want the three I had and they were mine. If it weren't for Frank all of them would have landed down in those dumpsters down by the docks."

"Oh stop, Tracy. You know you love those kids."

"Yeah, I do. Now. But Frank was the one the one that kept me from catching a 1-8-7 when those fools was growing up. There was nothing about the whole parenting thing that I liked. It was like I had been given a twenty year sentence for having sex. No, huh uh kids ain't for me. Ain't my thang... You're a better woman than me Mabel. But anyway I was just calling to tell you a few of the girls and I were going up to Massanutten for the week before New Years and thought you might like to join us."

"Now Tracy you know good and well I have these children and can't leave them alone. And you know damn well I can't find a babysitter for five kids for a week."

"Doesn't the county have a respite for foster parents? You know somewhere they can go when you're up to your head in it?"

"They do but the first time I used it they split each of my kid to a different home and they came back here with war stories and I thought I would have to get ‘em therapy for post traumatic stress so I just keep ‘em with me and tough it out.”

“And that’s exactly why we chose Massanutten. You can have your own cottage, the kids can come along and there are plenty of things for them to do. There’s skiing, tubing, swimming… You name it they have it. And I’m pretty sure they’d love to get out of the city and out of the house.”

“I don’t know with things the way they are. You know I’m on a fixed income. My pension and social security only goes so far with five kids. Everything is so touch and go right through here.”

“That’s why I’m giving you my time share and the rest of us are simply pooling our funds for another cabin but yours is free. Now how can you say no to that?”

“I guess I can’t,” Mabel said smiling. “I sure could use a break. A change of pace would be right on time right through here.”

“So you’ll go?”

“I suppose so. Let me run it past the kids when they get home. Make sure they don’t have anything planned.”

“Okay. Call me back. In the meantime I’ll check with Frank and see if he can’t get your van in for a tune up in the next couple of days.”

"Okay. Talk to you later Trace." Mabel said hanging up the phone.

The two women had been close friends since they entered the post office together more than twenty years ago and had planned everything together. Family vacations when their kids were young and had become more like sisters than friends over the years. But as Tracy had enjoyed the fruits of her labors following their retirement Mabel's life had done just the opposite.

Six months after retirement Mabel went for her yearly check up.

"So, Mabel now that you've officially retired how do you plan on spending all this free time you'll have on your hands," Dr. Ali said to his patient of twenty years.

"You know I've never really thought about it. I've always wanted to travel. Saved up a little and with Henry's passing there's not much else for me to do. Guess I'll just kick my feet up and read and enjoy a glass of Merlot every now and then."

"Sounds like a plan. Well, you enjoy the rest of your day Mabel and I'll be in touch just as soon as I get the lab work back but from what I can see you look to be as fit as a fiddle. How old are you now Mabel."

"Sixty seven."

"Are you serious? My God woman you don't look a day over thirty five. You haven't changed a day since the first time you walked into this office!"

“Thanks doc,” Mabel said smiling. “You certainly know the right things to say to a woman.”

“I’m being honest. You know Black women don’t age like other women.”

“They may not physically but I certainly feel every bit of sixty seven. I have no energy and I’m tired all the time.”

“Do I have you on a vitamin regime?”

“Not that I know of…”

“Well let’s do that after I get the test results back and perhaps change your diet.”

“If it’s going to give me some more energy then I’m all for it.”

“Okay. Well, on your way out tell Felicia to schedule you for the same time next week and we’ll look at a vitamin regiment and tweaking your diet and see if that helps.”

“Sounds good,” Mabel said as she slid off the table. “Until next week then,” Mabel said shaking Dr. Ali’s hand.

The following week brought an unexpected twist as Mabel entered the doctor’s office.

“Mrs. Gibson will you follow me,” the tall, buxom Felicia said. Mabel followed. “Dr. Ali will be with you in a minute.”

"Thank you."

Moments later Dr. Ali appeared just as clean and neat as ever. Boy, that man had a way of putting his clothes together in just such a way that he reeked of money and good taste.

"Afternoon, Mabel," Dr. Ali said extending his hand.

"Dr. Ali."

The doctor sat down across from Mabel and sighed.

"Well Mabel. We received the results from your blood work with some rather disturbing results."

"Oh goodness," Mabel whispered loud enough for the doctor to hear. "Is it bad doctor?"

"Well, it's not good but it's nothing that we can't manage. Your blood pressure and cholesterol are a little high but manageable. What concerns me is your sugar level which is quite high as well as you're A1C levels."

"What's that mean in layman's talk?"

"I think we're looking at diabetes Mabel."

Mabel, speechless simply stared at the doctor waiting for the punch line. When he didn't deliver one she grinned broadly.

"Are you okay Mabel?"

"Yes doctor. Despite your prognosis I'm really quite fine. Why do you ask?"

"Well, in all of my years practicing medicine I've never seen quite that reaction? Diabetes is a serious medical issue and that's not to say that it cannot be treated and controlled but it is a serious medical issue that can be life threatening if not treated and dealt with appropriately."

"Believe me doctor I know. I can probably tell you as much about it as you know. My mother's side of the family are all diabetics. My mother was a diabetic and I've always known that it was genetic and there was a good chance that I would get it sooner or later. That's not what I was smiling at."

"What then?"

"Have you ever heard the saying that man makes plans and God laughs?"

"No. I can't say that I have."

"Well, now you have. And remember it doctor as you plan your life. Twenty years ago my kids were graduating from high school and on their way to college. Henry and I were happy and planning how to convert the kids room into a den and a library and enclose the patio in back so we could share each other on those warm summer nights in privacy. We were getting ready to enjoy each other again and after raising two beautiful children it was our time. We were going to travel to those exotic islands we'd always read and dreamed about when there was no money. We finally had a little nest egg and everything looked grand. And then God laughed. I went in to wake Henry up one Saturday morning for breakfast and there was no Henry. He'd passed away in his sleep. Coroner said it was a massive heart attack but I know it was simply him working, planning to live. He worked himself to death.

I survived Henry's death. And that wasn't easy. You see Henry was more than a husband. He was my best and only friend. But I survived. I had to reinvent my world. And I did. And just when I had finally regrouped and gotten over his loss and started getting comfortable and used to living alone and really, really enjoying my retirement He laughed again. And gave me five children and here I am starting all over again. I'm sixty seventy years old with a new born and four others all under sixteen with no help. And I am so tired and see no end in sight.

Only recourse I have is to come to you and ask for you to give me some energy so I can continue doing the Lord's work."

"Mabel you've worked hard your entire life. There's no reason that at your age you shouldn't be tired."

"I'm aware of that doctor. But I had to laugh with Him this time. It just seems so ironic that I came to you seeking some time type or remedy for life; something to pick me up and rejuvenate me and you add some more weight to my burdens," she said laughing. "I don't know how much more I can carry."

"The Lord only gives you what you can bear," Dr. Ali said staring at this woman he had known for most of his adult life. He watched as she grew older in front of him and knew he had no prescription for what ailed her. Life had a funny way of tearing the spirit down and there was little to do to revive it once despair set in.

"Anyway I've prescribed you a couple of medications which should help you're your cholesterol and high blood pressure. And I'm prescribing Metformin for the diabetes. Dr. Ali went on to tell her about changing her diet and getting plenty of exercise but most of it fell on deaf ears. She was just so tired.

That was six months ago and things had hardly changed. Perhaps the trip to Massanutten would be just the change she needed. Maybe Tracy was right. And it would be great for the kids too. These days she worried more and more about Malik. He was still a good boy but at sixteen he seemed preoccupied with the streets and there were so many dangers nowadays.

Between the drugs, the gang violence and babies walking around with babies she feared for Malik and he seemed drawn to it like metal to a magnet. She tried to find alternatives but even with ball he found a way to spend any spare time hanging out.

The Hill District had been pretty affluent area for Black folks when she was growing up and Pittsburgh's jazz center but it was now as rough if not rougher than any other urban area in the city. Shootings were so common an occurrence on the Hill that they seldom made Channel 4 News anymore. And she worried about Malik being out there in the mix but those little wanna be street thugs made so much more of an impression than his sixty seven yea old aunt and in the end she realized and resigned herself to the fact that here was little she could do.

Monique a year younger than Malik posed a different set of problems but to Mabel they were just as serious perhaps even more so. Monique reminded Mabel of her sister Gretta. Always a quiet child neither Monique nor Gretta could ever be seen as a problem until that one day when fourteen year old Gretta came home and told mommy that she was pregnant.

Only a week ago Mabel had returned from grocery shopping to find Monique and some little snotty nosed hard head with the lights off and half dressed. No telling what may have happened if she'd stopped by Tracy's to pick up the muffin tins. And if it was one thing that Mabel didn't need it was another mouth to feed.

The young girl tried to ease her aunt's fear.

"We were just kissing auntie."

"Looked like a lot more than that to me."

"He would like for it to be but that's all it was auntie and that's as far as it goes."

"You say that but I've seen a kiss turn into a family more than a few times in my life."

"I hear you auntie but you don't have to worry about anything to worry here auntie."

"I certainly hope not young lady." But worry she did and at times she wondered if she weren't more concerned about these children than she'd been wither own.

The two twins were a handful as well. Mabel had long since stopped hanging up her coat in the hall closet choosing to leave on the Queen Ann chair in the foyer that way when the phone rang in the middle of her soaps as did at least two or three times a week she could simply grab it and go. When the phone rang around mid-day she wouldn't even bother to answer it but would grab her coat and head to the school. Most of the time the twins would have tag team matches with some poor, little, helpless child that may have stared at them a second too long and now was sitting right outside Principal Thurman's office nose bloody, clothes ripped waiting for mom t pick him up.

It was all a bit much for the sixty seven year old who had never done anything but walked the straight and narrow and planned on spinning her waning days on some tropical island in the Caribbean.

Now with Gretta having chosen to abandon her children for the leisurely life of a state funded sabbatical Mabel's life had taken a turn to. Perhaps Masanutten would be a welcome break from the everyday drudgery her life had turned into. And so without even consenting the children Mabel packed them all into the van turned he GPS on and headed down the Pennsylvania Turnpike. Six hours later she saw Tracy's Camry in front of the welcome center.

Tracy waved eagerly when she saw Mabel.

“It’s so good to see you,” she said sticking her head into the window of the van. “I really didn’t think you were going to make it,” she said waving at the kids and pinching the baby’s cheek. “Hey darling.”

“Told you I’d be here.”

“Okay. Well let’s go get settled in so we can stat enjoying the festivities.”

“I gotta go to the bathroom auntie,” one of the twins said.

“Where are we Aunt Mabel?” Malik said wiping the sleep from his eyes.

“In the woods,” Monique answered. “This looks like the perfect setting for one of those horror movies on Syfy.”

“Oh, hush you all. Don’t knock it before you try it. Besides it’s a change from that asphalt jungle you call home. A change is good.”

“Do people actually live out here?” Malik asked innocently enough.

“No. Not here. This is a resort where people come to vacation but there are communities where people live very similar to this.”

“Why auntie? Why would anyone want to live out here in the boonies? There’s nothing to do.”

"Let's give it a couple of days and then we'll talk again. Okay guys?" Aunt Mabel said as she pulled in front of a log cabin deep in the woods.

"Grab the bags Malik."

"Watch my bags Malik! My make ups in them," Monique yelled.

"All the make up in the world wouldn't help that ugly mug of yours. If Yogi Bear saw you he'd do an about face and give himself up to the forest ranger," Malik laughed.

"Real funny Malik. Real funny."

"Goodness! Is that all you two do? You're worst than a bunch of two year olds. Now grab the bags and come on."

The twins were already in a spirited snowball fight when an errant throw hit the toddler clinging to Mabel's coattails flush in the face leaving a deep crimson mark on the baby's face and knocking her to the ground. The toddler screamed in pain.

Mabel horrified dropped the luggage and bent down and picked up the screaming toddler in an effort to comfort her.

"You two get your butts in the house," Mabel said her heart racing. She could feel her blood pressure rising.

Glaring at the two boys Mabel knew if she said anything it would be ugly and refrained from saying anything.

The glare said enough and the twins scurried in the house.

Malik and Monique rushed inside and ran to the baby's side.

"You alright sweetie," Monique said rushing to the baby's side and then searching her aunt's eyes. She knew Aunt Mabel was tired and each day she cared for them was a struggle. Monique loved her aunt dearly and could feel the weight her brothers and sisters were putting on the old woman.

"Grab my pocketbook sweetie and hand my medicine."

This always bothered Malik. In his anger he turned to the twins.

"Sit your little narrow asses down and shut up. I hear a peep out of either one of you I'm going to beat both your asses," he yelled in anger.

The twins not used to their older brother addressing in such a manner climbed onto the sofa and dropped their heads. Both boys adored Malik and hated the idea of their older being angry with them.

Malik didn't have to look twice to know that they were sitting quietly. He hardly if ever raised his voice but he loved his Aunt Mabel and refused to see her hut or in pain.

"You alright auntie?" Malik asked his concern showing as he found a pillow and propped it up behind her head and grabbed her hand.

"I'm fine Malik," she said in an attempt to comfort he nephew. "Don't yell at those boys," she whispered into Malik's ear. "They're just children."

Malik shot a warning glance at the boy's who were now slapping each other playfully.

"Don't let me have to speak to you again!"

The boys sat straight up and folded their hands in their lap.

Mabel said nothing but was thankful for Malik's help. She had enough to do without having to constantly chastise the two boys who didn't seem content unless they were fighting or were involved in some kind of mischief.

A knock at the door of the cabin broke the tense silence.

"So how y'all doing. You all like it?"

"Kids are adjusting," Mabel said forcing a smile.

"What's wrong with y'all? Seems like someone died up in here. Y'all s'pozed to be having a good time. What's wrong?"

"Marquis hit the baby in the face with a snowball."

"I did not. Marcus hit her."

Malik slapped the nine year old hard across the mouth.

"If Aunt Mabel said you threw the damn snowball then you threw it.

Don't you ever sass her! Do you hear me?"

Marquis shook his head as the tears rolled down his face.

"Malik!" Mabel yelled. "I can handle this."

"Sorry auntie. I didn't mean to upset you,"

Malik said rearranging the pillow to make his aunt more comfortable.

"Anyway, we're still trying to get settled in but I love the place.

I can really see someone coming here to get away from it all and just relax. It's so peaceful."

"Too peaceful if you ask me," Monique countered.

"No one's asking you and you need to learn to stay out of grown folk's conversations," Monique shouted at Malik.

"Whew! Lordy! Mabel you're a better woman than I am," Tracy remarked.

"I don't know who died and made you boss," Monique snapped.

"Hey! Hey! Stop all that damn noise! This trip was supposed to give your Aunt Mabel a chance to get away and relax and here you are causing her even more stress."

Everyone was quiet now.

"You know what? Don't unpack a thing. Just grab your bags and come with me."

The children turned to their aunt who said nothing.

"I don't know what you're looking at Mabel for. You weren't thinking about her when you were creating chaos and running her pressure up. So don't be lookin' at her now. Now pick up your shit and go get in the car," Tracy said staring at each child who grabbed their belongings and headed out the door. "Mabel I'll be back in a few minutes. Just give me a chance to get them settled in. The girls and I'll handle this shit," she said wrapping up the baby who reached for her aunt and began to cry. "Don't worry Mabel. There's four of us and five kids. We'll handle this with no problem."

"Thanks Trace. They're good kids. They've just been through a lot."

"And who hasn't but I'm not going to sit around and let these little heathens kill my best friend. Shit, they're not even your responsibility and if that sorry ass sister of yours didn't care enough to take care of them I'll be damn if I would."

"Ahhh Tracy. Don't say that. You know you don't mean that."

"The hell if I don't, she said wrapping the crying baby up. "Hush gal!" Then turning to Mabel she saw the utter exhaustion in her face.

"You get some rest Mabel. I'll send Malik over in about an hour to make sure you're situated and have everything you need," she said pushing Mabel back in the recliner and handing her the remote. "You hungry?"

"No. I'm fine Trace. Just need a nap and I'll be good as new."

"Okay you rest. We have the bungalow three doors down so if you need anything—anything at all—you just call."

"Thanks so much. You're a godsend."

Mabel heard the door close. It was snowing harder now. Mabel turned the recliner around to stare out and see the big, fluffy fakes cascading to the already covered ground and closed her eyes for the last time.

King of Courts

"What up Blackman?"

"Chillin'," Dante said bumping chests with Sorvino.

"Cold as a bitch out here today."

"You ain't never lied. Sorvino said going in his jacket pocket and pulling out a pint of Paul Masson. "Here hit this anti-freeze. Should warm you up a little bit," he said hitting the bottle before passing it on.

The November wind had a bite usually reserved for the end of December or early January.

"Gonna be a cold winter."

"Who you tellin'? I'm seriously considerin' going up to Bronx Community College and enrolling. Nigga gittin' to be too old to be just hangin'out."

"You's a funny dude. We been hangin' on this same corner since we was just pee wees and one day you gonna tell me you just gonna change your whole life?"

"Brotha gotta do what a brotha gotta do. Ain't no future in these streets. Nothin' out here but death and drama and I seen enough to know I wants no parts of either."

"I hear ya. But what's a brotha gonna do? It ain't like I can parlay this education into a job and damn sure ain't joining Obama's war. Just ain't a lot of options for a nigga nowadays."

"You could always enroll in school."

"Ain't like you got a lot of alternatives. It's been a while since I seen anybody down here trying' to sign you to a ten day contract."

It was true. Two years ago at six seven Malik Sorvino had been one of the top small forwards in New York City prep history and was thought a sure fire NBA prospect but a sheisty agent who assured him of his pro status bilked both colleges and the pros out of thousands. When the dust had settled Malik Sealy at seventeen who had only a few months ago had been as hot as the new Apple phones was now for all intensive purposes blackballed from the one thing he loved most.

Nowadays he resigned himself to hangin' out with lifelong friend Dante Williams but as another winter blew in off the East River he realized as he looked around that there was little difference between himself and Willie the Wino. He had always prided himself as an athlete and never taken an interest in drinking and smoking. Nothing to ham the body that would take him to that million dolla payday. But those days were long gone now and he was no more than another lost soul hangin' out on the avenue all dreams deferred. Every now and then some hot shot would show up at the park and after a good deal of prodding he'd go down, pick up the gauntlet and let them know after raining threes on them that he was still King of Rucker Park even if he didn't have some lofty shoe contract to recognize him. But picking up a b-ball was just too hard for him now. It bought so many good and bad memories and now he only wished he had listened to Coach McGuire. But the coach's voice was just a whisper amongst the crowds that cheered loudly and egged him on to bypass college, get an agent and go pro.

Where were they now?

Like every high school star he had aspirations. He'd watched his father literally work himself to death trying to raise his seven brothers and sisters on a municipal worker's salary and die at the ripe old age of forty eight of a heart attack. And being the next to the oldest and the oldest male he had just naturally taken on the mantle of head of household. The money he made playing ball for the high rollers at least made life that much more bearable for now or so he thought. In a couple of years and with a lucrative

NBA contract his moms would no longer have to work and he could easily take care of his brothers and sisters. And then all had gone haywire.

"Man you could go to Bronx Community College as a walk on or even go to a junior college for a year or two. By that time, all the hullabaloo will have blown over and some Division I school will have noticed you and you'll be right back on track and heading for the bigs. The talent is still there. But son you're wasting it hanging out on these corners," Dante said handing Malik the bottle.

"I hear you."

"I want you to do more than just hear me son. I'll be waiting on you by the subway at 8 a.m. Don't let me down son. We been out here for close to two years and seen all there is to see. Ain't nothin' happenin'. Let's make this move so. 8 a.m. Don't let me down son," Dante said before chest bumping him again. "Here hit this one last time before I roll," he said passing the bottle to his boy. "8 a.m. baby,"

Malik and Dante had grown up together and were inseparable since before they could remember and Malik didn't have a sibling he considered any closer than Dante. They had been hardship and wars together and had always been there for each other but this thing Dante wanted Malik troubled him. They'd played ball together since grade school with Dante doing the majority of the dirty work while Malik took the accolades. And when the walls came tumbling down it was Malik who felt the brunt of it. Now here was Dante saying 'two tears in a bucket and say fuck it' but it just wasn't that easy for Malik. No one was pointing the finger at Dante saying he fraudently duped the major colleges and pros out of hundreds of thousands of dollars. No, they blamed him even though he hadn't received a pittance.

He could go with Dante in the morning and Lord knows Dante was right. Wasn't nothing good going to come to anyone standing on the corners of Harlem. But... there was always that but...

It hadn't been this cold in Lord knows how long. The old radiator hissed and banged and did everything it could to emit as much heat as it could. The apartment still had a frosty chill to it and Malik wondered if it could be any colder outside than in the tiny two bedroom apartment. Momma was already up and dressed for work. His older Shana was up too fixing oatmeal for the twins.

"Malik is that you baby?"

"Yes momma," he mumbled.

"What do you have planned for today?"

"I was thinking about going up to Bronx Community College and enroll for the semester."

Miss Sorvino stopped dead in her tracks, put her pocketbook on the couch and turned to face her oldest son. She then reached and grabbed her son hugging him tightly. A tear ran down her cheek.

"I've waited two years to hear something along those lines son. I was so worried you were just gonna become another statistic," she said looking up. Thank you so much Lord."

"Ahh momma. Won't nothing gonna happen to me. I ain't caught up in the streets like that."

"Bullets ain't got no names and just as many innocent people get killed by stray bullets as those they're intended for."

"Ahh, momma. You worry too much," Malik said smiling and kissing his momma on the cheek.

"You better listen to momma Junior. You don't get to be old being no fool," his sister Shana chimed in wiping the twin's mouths and buttoning their coats.

"I hear you," Malik said. "Let me get outta here. I'm supposed to meet Dante at the subway by eight."

"Well, you'd better shake a tail feather. It's a quarter to eight now," Shana said smacking Malik on the back of the head. "Good luck baby brother."

Malik bounded the three flights of stairs and out into the streets where he found the weather warmer than in the apartment. It was still bitter cold. The five minute walk to the subway seemed like forever with the cold bitter wind whipping his face. Pulling the hat down over his ears and buttoning the top button on his coat Malik Sorvino hastened his pace. He knew that if Dante had waited for him he would be down on the platform out of the cold.

Bounding down the stairs once more Malik jumped the turnstiles and saw his best friend Dante in his usual place at the far end of the platform.

"What's up Blackman?" Dante said smiling and hugging Malik. "Wasn't sure if you were going to show or not."

"Me either. But when I ran it past momma her eyes lit up so that I just couldn't let her down."

"It's the smart move."

"Beats this fucking cold. Least I won't be spending the winter outside in the cold."

"Whatever. How about your dumbass has another chance to get this shit right. You might even get an education son."

In minutes the train came to a grinding halt. The two men disembarked and ran up the steps. Bronx Community College loomed large and formidable before them. Once inside Malik's eyes widened as he watched the students scurry before him. A cute, little Puerto Rican girl winked as she passed and Malik broke out in a full fledged grin showing every tooth in his mouth.

"Hey bro, I think I'm gonna like this shit," he commented.

"Thought you would. Come on we need to find admissions."

"Excuse me miss," Malik said to a cute little brown skin hottie. "Can you show me where admissions is?" The girl smiled and began to give Malik directions.

"No ma'am," he said cutting the young lady off in mid sentence. Looking puzzled she stared up at him confused. "No ma'am. You see I'm directionally challenged. If you could show me the way then I'm sure I could find my way the next time."

"You're something," she said smiling.

"The name's Sorvino."

"That's an odd first name," she said smiling.

"No ma'am. My first name is actually Malik but around the way most people just call me Sorvino."

"Used to be this kid from uptown, he was a baller, he was all over the paper's was supposed to be the next LeBron. You any relation to him?"

"One and the same," Dante piped up.

"Well, you certainly are tall enough to be him," the girl chirped. "But I thought you were headed to the NBA?"

"He still is. Just got a little sidetracked," Dante intervened.

"And who's this? Your agent or your lawyer?"

"The name's Dante ma'am and I act as both as well as bodyguard and bff," Dante smiled sticking out his hand. "But I don't believe we got your name."

"Michelle. Michelle White. I don't know why you didn't go to the NBA but it's still good to see you doing something positive with your lives. You going to play ball for BCC? They could use all the help they can get. They're sorry as hell."

"Don't think so. I think we're just gonna concentrate on the books for right now," Malik said sorry for the attention he'd drawn.

"Really nice to see a brother with his priorities in order. Hope to see you around Malik Sorvino," she said turning and sashaying down the hall.

"What about me?"

"Yeah, you too bff."

"She was a cutie," Malik remarked randomly. "I think I could get to know her better."

"Slow your roll son. You don't step in every hole you see. Slow your roll. You're gonna see a lot finer honeys so don't go gettin' hooked up yet. But I like that shit you threw on her about you concentratin' on the books instead of ball. Nice touch son."

"I'm serious D. I've seen how easily they can take away your dreams but they can't take away your education and it's a sure thing. Besides I can blow out a knee at any time but I'll always have my degree to fall back on."

"You right but don't eliminate ball altogether. It can still be an avenue to a lot of other things."

"I'll keep that in mind, holmes" Malik responded as they stood in line.

An hour and a half later both young men headed back down the subway steps. Once on the crowded train Dante turned to Malik.

"We are officially college students."

Malik smiled.

"Bad as I wanted to get out of high school I can't believe I just went and enrolled."

"Ain't a whole lot of options out here for a nigga."

"Word, son."

Malik found Bronx Community easier than high school. There wasn't the pressure of carrying the basketball program's winning tradition on and for once he could just concentrate on his classes. And Dante had been right. There was no need to rush into anything with the ladies. He had met a dozen o so just in class. Most of whom knew nothing of his basketball prowess. All in all it had been a good move and with Shana's tutoring he maintained a B average in all of his classes. But there was something missing and if he didn't recognize it Dante did.

"Follow me son. Wanta introduce you to someone," Figuring it was just another cutie Malik fell into the quick step. Moments later he was surprised to be facing a towering hulk of a man.

"Malik, this is Coach T. I told coach how you loved ball and he agreed to let us scrimmage with the team."

"Your friend Dante here tells me that you're interested in scrimmaging with the team. And to be honest I was against it but he was so persistent I thought it easier to just let you run than to have him come in here every day touting your high flying act."

"You have to see him play Coach. I'm telling you he's the best two guard/small forward in New York City."

"C'mon man," Malik said cutting a warning look in Dante's direction. "I have even laced up a pair of Nike's in months."

"There's a couple of pair of clean sweats on the chair in my office."

"I'm gonna beat you skinny, narrow ass when this is over," Malik said shooting a wary glance at Dante.

Dante laughed.

"You were starting to get a pouch like your daddy used to have. And you know the honeys don't like no dudes with pouches."

"Fuck you holmes. I told you the day we registered I was only interested in one thing and one thing only and that was coming here on the d/l and getting an education. That's it. I ain't tryna be Billy Basketball no more. I just wanna chill is all."

"Ain't nobody asking you to sign no contract. All I was asking Coach was if you could scrimmage so you could play against some halfway decent competition in a nice warm gym. What the fuck is wrong with that. Are you ready?"

"Yeah," Malik grumbled.

Ten minutes later, both men were dripping sweat and a small crowd had formed at the door of the gym as Dante led the break. Malik came in from the left wing and soared high above his defender. Dante turned his head away before lofting a perfect no look pass which Malik slammed through. The crowd at the door murmured and there was soon a buzz that spread through the campus of Bronx Community College.

Two weeks later, Coach T. made Malik Sorvino a proposition. And though it was a long way from an NBA contract Malik with Dante's prompting accepted. The high flying act of Dante Williams and Malik Sorvino soon became known as DMS and the school's empty gym suddenly became packed to capacity with standing room only for practices.

Tomorrow was the first game of the season and despite his objections to playing no one was looking any more forward to it than Malik. Well, that is except for Dante who was playing opposite him at power forward.

Donning the crimson and gold uniforms Malik looked over and winked at Dante before they took the court. Sixty minutes later, a new chapter had been born at Bronx Community College where Malik Sorvino had been coronated king.

The Retreat

Eighteen year Innocence was a mess. At five foot eight and gorgeous she was just finishing up her senior year in high school and had the world at her feet or so she thought.

Here she was built like a brick house, breasts not too big and not too small like ripe melons and an ass that called men, grown men, close to fifty years of age to her like metal to a magnet.

For eighteen, Innocence had a pretty good head on her shoulders. Though a little arrogant and somewhat conceited by her bless-ed good looks her parents had made sure she understood that she had nothing to do with her physical beauty and if there was anyone responsible for her looks it was them and the good Lord above not her.

A year or so earlier the young thugs she called classmates and what they thought were all that mattered to her but now with the possibility of college fast becoming a reality her focus shifted. Now no longer did her phone ring constantly or did her texting matter so much. Now all that mattered was how well she did on her SAT's and if she could hang in there with the track team just long enough to letter in the sport so she could add it to her transcripts so she could present a rather formidable resume to A&T.

Innocence choice of colleges had never really been in doubt and I don't know if it were the years of attending homecomings or the fact that her favorite aunt had attended and both her parents had worked there at one time or another. Her mother was still in the college's employ and had been for the past ten or fifteen years. And they were both there now as she got ready to board the bus. She had never been on a retreat before but when her parents suggested she take a break from her studies she agreed even though she hated the idea of going on a religious retreat of sorts.

As Innocence boarded the bus, she was confronted by a rather well-dressed man she had to say was around her father's age sporting a bald head.

"Glad to have you among us young lady. Don't see too many young people on a retreat such as this," he said smiling and helping her with the oversized suitcase mommy had insisted on her taking.

"Thank you. It's nice to be here," she said matter-of-factly not meaning a word of it. The well dressed man paid her little mind.

Seemingly well-known by all in attendance the rather debonair, brown-skinned, middle-aged man with the well chiseled face, and meticulously trimmed, salt and pepper mustache and beard found himself caught in deep thought. He could sense the mindless teen had no more inkling to be there than he did but in his desperation to get away from the maddening crowd he'd taken the advice of his friend, an older woman whose advice he'd always revered but now as he glanced around at the myriad of passengers he began to wonder about her wisdom and the fallibility of her reasoning.

He'd been caught up in the deafening chattering of women allvying for his time and hand in marriage when all he wanted to do was give time to his craft. It had gotten to the point where his phone rang constantly and every time he had the time to draw a breath there was some woman there trying to breathe for him. If he didn't catch his breath soon he was sure he would suffocate and die at the hands of those who claimed they loved him most.

Many years before when barely an adult he'd suffered just the opposite problem and gone to his father to seek advice. His father had instructed him, now in his late teens to forget about women.

'Women have been here since the beginning of mankind. And they will be here until the end of mankind. You never have to worry about acquiring a woman. All you have to worry about is the type of woman you acquire. But the better your lot in life, the better the woman you will acquire. If you want a smart and astute woman then work on improving your mind. Likes attract and a smart woman wants a smart man.'

And so had enrolled in and attended the university but unlike most who attended simply for the purposes of procuring employment he attended for the sole purpose of improving himself. He soon joined the Muslim religion, changed his name and began the long journey into understanding himself and the world in which he lived. He read and studied the great writers and philosophers with the hopes that he would gain a better insight into what made him tick and those around him.

Following his graduation, Knowledge as he was now known, continued his studies having now gained the discipline to author a novel on his own. To his surprise the novel met with critical acclaim and after much prompting by his publicist Knowledge went on his first book tour and not only met with a fair share of financial success but something he hardly expected. There were women by the dozens. The old man had been right once again. Improve yourself and your self-esteem and all else will fall in line.

Well, they had certainly come. And in droves. At book signings, press conferences and just sitting at a bar women now approached.

His novel considered by the media to be urban fiction and which targeted Black women, although that was not his intent at the inception, brought women from all walks of life. And not only Black women but brown, beige, white and yellow clamored to get to know the author.

All that it took was for Knowledge to improve his lot in life. Now anywhere he went he was sure to stand among the many faithful supporters and admirers. But it had all gotten to be a little bit out of control and when Duchess suggested a retreat he'd jumped at the opportunity.

Knowledge stood at the front of the bus warily, looking over the passengers. His eyes seemed to adjust to the cloudy, overcast sky on this December evening when he was struck by a young brother all in disarray looking quite disheveled. He was quite a contrast to the rest of the impeccably and casually dressed riders that Knowledge began to at once try to put the pieces together. He was quite curious to know the young man's story. He wondered why such a good-looking young brother had seen fit to let himself go like this. And as tired and as worn as Knowledge was he knew that if there was anybody in need of a respite it was this young man.

Looking no more than twenty seven or twenty eight at best the young man who could have been Knowledge's son wore a sagging, faded pair of those expensive designer jeans young folks seem so fond of. I believe they're called True Religion, Coogi or something along those lines, a pair of Timberland boots that had long ago seen better days and were turned over so badly about the heel that he seemed slew footed and a University of Tennessee goose down jacket that had long ago gone out of style along with a

Carolina blue University of North Carolina fitted cap. And where everyone else seemed anxious, alive and expectantly upbeat this young man who it would have seemed to possess the most upside of any of the retreaters with all of his youth and promise hardly seemed to appear so but was in fact rather distant and morose.

At around this time when Knowledge had all but given up trying to guess the young man's story a thirtyish looking couple wearing tan colored suits which somehow complimented each other nicely pulled up alongside the bus and were discharged from a shiny black Lincoln Navigator by their chauffeur.

Getting out the tall, stately Black gentleman so nattily attired smiled broadly as he took his wife's hand and helped her from the SUV leading her through the thinning crowd speaking ever so cordially to the sixty or seventy retreaters. Approaching the disheveled young man who appeared more homeless than the typical passenger gave the minister time to take pause and take a second look.

"Reverend Goode," the man in the beige leisure suit said extending his hand as he'd done several dozen times previously although now he did it with some apprehension and reservation.

"Hopeless," the young man replied.

"Is that your birth name?" The good reverend inquired.

"Not sure," the man replied. "It's all I've ever known."

Not sure of what to make of the man the good reverend continued making his way through the crowd until he came to a woman that again peeked his attention.

Dressed in six inch pumps, her hair sat high atop her head in a tight bun and her horned rimmed glasses gave one the first impression of a school marm. Yet, on closer observation she was certainly no school marm. A low cut red dress showing more than ample cleavage while a rose colored tattoo adorned her left breast which was now partially exposed for the good reverend to see.

Glancing down one couldn't help but notice the red fish net stockings exposing the most beautiful, and sultry, chocolate thighs the good reverend had ever had the pleasure of seeing.

"Thank God" he muttered to himself, "for small blessings Lord."

It was the good reverend's wife, no slouch herself who made it a point to intervene noticing the bedazzled look on her husband's face.

"Mrs. Goode," she said extending her hand, "...certainly glad you could join us."

"Harlot. Harlot Rousse," the woman said.

Mrs. Goode forced a smile but was hardly happy to have the woman on the trip. She could spot trouble a mile away and this woman was trouble. Still, and aside from this she had to admit that she was somewhat amused or rather taken back by such an interesting congregation of people.

When everyone had boarded and was seated the bus driver boarded and started the engine. Easing away from the curb all heads turned to the sounds of screams.

"Hold the bus.! Hold the bus!" A rather large man well over three hundreds came lumbering up alongside banging on the door. "The name's Wisdom for all those that don't know me," he said doing his best to catch his breath and talk at the same time. "What is it they say he said heading down the aisle and searching for a seat.

"Better late than never," he grunted as the bus headed off with a lurch.

Innocence only prayed that that dirty hobo she heard someone refer to as Hopeless wouldn't grab the empty seat next to her. Sure, she had to admit he was a pretty nice looking guy if you could get beyond the matted dreads that looked as if they hadn't seen water in a year.

She tried to return the gesture and exhaled at the same time giving thanks and praise that he had passed her by. Innocence swore she could smell him but didn't have time to dwell on the homeless man when...

"Hey Miss Thang. How you doin'? Name's Butter. Butter Love. What's yours?"

"Innocence," she replied taken aback by the woman's coarse demeanor.

"Seat taken?"

"No ma'am." Innocence said giving the woman the once over.

"Well, I guess it is now," she said smiling.

Innocence wondered if Miss Thang or Butter Love or whatever the hell she called herself had had a chance to see herself in the mirror before leaving the house this morning. There was too much mascara, rouge and the false eyelashes were way too much. Mama had always told her that sometimes less was more. It was obvious Butter hadn't gotten the memo.

"So whatcha do girl?"

"Nothing right now. I'm still in high school. Just getting ready to go to college. I start A&T in the fall providing I get in. And you Mrs. Love," Innocence asked the older woman more out of politeness than anything else.

"I'm in customer service baby girl. I went to A&T a couple of semesters myself and damn near starved to death so I took a couple of semesters off and went down to Twiggy's and danced to earn some extra money. I didn't quit or give up though. It was just hard. I didn't qualify for financial aid and it was hard trying to pay tuition, eat and have a place to live but I went back. I just didn't go back to 'T'. Just couldn't afford it so I switched up and went to a little two year community college for the next nine years and I'm only six credits short of getting my associates degree in business." Butter said smiling.

"That's really great Mrs. Love. A degree in business should really help you in your field."

The older woman laughed.

"I see why they call you Innocence. You're a little naive aren't you," she said pulling out a small flask and sipping. "Baby girl, I'm in customer service. It's one of the only fields where the more experience you have the more it hurts your career."

"So, what you're saying is that a college degree don't actually help you in your field? Is that what you're saying?" Innocence asked somewhat puzzled. For as long as she could remember education was a mandatory and necessary component if you were Black and wanted to succeed but here was someone with a different perspective.

"That's not to say that you shouldn't go to school. At your age a degree is mandatory." Innocence breathed a sigh of relief. She would have hated to ride for the next three hours next to someone who didn't value or see the importance of education when she'd been told all her life that education was the gateway to the stars. "Ya feel me? As long as we're in this recession there really ain't too many options open. College is without a doubt your best bet. Yes ma'am until Obama does something about the economy ain't much for nobody to do. He done bailed

Wall Street out and GM is selling cars at a record pace but up on 150th and 8th ain't much changed. It's even playing havoc with my business."

"How's that Mrs. Love?" The woman had Innocence ear now.

"Well, I have about twenty to twenty five loyal customers a week who always seem to help me make it through the rough spots. I mean these motherfuckers are high rollers down on Wall Street and bank managers, stock brokers. You get the picture and when they can't get away they still make sure Butter Love is taken care of. But girl if it weren't for them loyal bastards and their affinity for the best pussy in Harlem I might be flippin' burgers in Mickey D's."

Just then it dawned on Innocence that Butter Love was a hooker, a prostitute, a call girl no more than a common street walker, a ho.

Innocence dropped her head to her chest and hoped it wasn't too obvious but knew she had turned crimson red from embarrassment. Biting down hard on her lower lip her mind raced. 'I thought this was a retreat, a time for reflection and to be introspective, a time for deep thought, inner thought,' she mused to herself. At least that's what her parent's told her. It was a time for people to get to know themselves and to become closer in their relationship with God. Instead she'd run into the 'mouth-of-the-South'.

"Here! You want some honey?" Butter said passing her the flask.

"No. No, thank you Ms. Love," pushing the flask away. 'Ain't no telling where this foul mouth woman's mouth has been.' Innocence thought to herself. The liquor only seemed to spark Butter as she erupted spewing racial epitaphs about every red-necked, hillbilly, hunky cracker that had opposed Obama from Ted Cruz to John Boehner and leaving no one out calling Hillary a dyke and commenting that Hilary wasn't mad at Bill but was happy Monica got down on her knees and Hillary was going to personally give Monica a medal and some knee pads just as soon as she got into the White House for serving her country and saving her the trouble since men go against Hilary's very constitution... dyke that she is. Even Innoence had to chuckle once or twice as every head on the bus seemed to turn to see what all the commotion was about.

When the tirade had all but ended Innocence couldn't help but wonder if maybe Stinky or Hopeless or whatever the hell his name was would have made for a better riding partner. He certainly couldn't have been worse. At least he was quiet.

"Oh shit!" Butter said spilling the alcohol on her blouse. Heads turned. "Oh, Lord did I say something wrong?" she asked elbowing Innocence slightly. "I gotta keep reminding myself that I'm hangin' out with these born again, sanctified, Holy Roller motherfuckers. Shit, I ain't got this shit to do. Hey driver are you going to stop any time soon. Lord knows I need a cigarette."

Innocence dropped her head in embarrassment. She only hoped that no one would associate her with this foul mouthed woman.

The good reverend also known as Reverend Goode suddenly appeared almost out of nowhere like Moses to the Israelites to lead Innocence out of the torment she was in.

"Name's Reverend Goode ma'am and I'm conducting this retreat."

"Nice to meet you reverend. Sho, is nice to have such a good looking man running the damn thang." she said flirting openly now. "You know quite a few of my clients are ministers. Here let me give you one of my cards. Maybe we can do business sometime. Or maybe we can just have dinner and see where it goes from there. Give me a call sometime rev."

The good reverend was forced to smile.

"Ten years ago I might have taken you up on that Mrs. Love. But the Lord decided to step up and bless me with a beautiful wife and I've been hooked ever since. Don't think she would appreciate me seeing anyone quite as attractive as you. Might inflame the little green eyed monster," the good reverend said still smiling. " But for now I have to ask you to refrain from the use of profanity while on the bus. Some of our older church members seem a bit offended by your language."

Butter Love looked at the good reverend incredulously.

"I know you're not serious. I ain't say nothing to nobody to offend them. Me and Innocence just sitting here having a friendly chat. Nosy motherfuckers need to tend to their own business instead of being all up in our conversation. Ain't that right baby girl?"

Innocence smiled cordially.

"I knew I should have given this shit some more thought before going on some retreat with some fuckin' born again Christians. See, that's what I'm talkin' 'bout. Damn do-gooders always stickin' their nosy asses into something that doesn't concern them. Wasn't talkin' to nobody but the bus driver and my girl Innocence here and she ain't seem to mind."

Butter was on a roll now. And the more she thought about the good reverend and those goddamn self-righteous son-of-a-bitches the louder she became.

"Nobody's trying to be in your business Ms. Love. Just try to show a little respect and consideration for those around you. That's all I ask."

"Listen here reverend. The only reason I'm even considering your request is because I like you and you seem like a decent guy. I can really see you as a potential client." she said looking the reverend up and down with lascivious eyes. "And that's the only reason I'm not going to curse these bible totin' mf'ers out. But believe me that's the only reason. Did I give you my card?"

"Yes, you did and I appreciate that Ms. Love."

Pulling his sleeve she whispered into his ear.

"Well, that and the fact that you have a nice ass and Lord knows what Butter Love can do with that."

By this time Innocence had had enough.

"I'm going to sit in the back Mrs. Love where I can stretch out a little bit and take a nap. I'll be back."

"No problem sweetie," Butter said still staring at the good reverend's ass as he walked away.

Knowledge approached as Innocence squeezed by him and made her way to the back of the bus.

"Well, if she's going I don't imagine you'd mind me sitting here for a few minutes ma'am?" Knowledge said eager to get away from the cackling hens who had made it a point to a point to surround him in the back of the bus. Quickly doing away with the introductions Butter Love picked up the conversation as if she'd known the handsome, middle-aged brother all her life.

"What happened my brotha? Did you get tired of those old, Holy Roller, sanctified, hypocrites sweatin' you? Lord knows you must have that special gift. Women can smell a man who has that good good. It's like a sixth sense. Wakes up the animal instincts in them."

Knowledge laughed.

"Don't know about all that. I just think that there are so few brothas my age out here doing' somethin' positive and so many single women that basically a brotha doing anything--anything at all can have his pick of the litter and trust me there's something mighty beautiful sistas out here just waiting for a decent brotha Love."

"I know that's right. Shit. I work in customer service everyday and I'm gonna tell you the truth. I see fewer and fewer brothas everyday. Most of my clients are middle-aged white men. Black men are few and far between. At one point, I had to think back to the last relationship I had with a brotha and had to go back twelve years when I was in high school. And let me tell you K. the majority of my clients are men. I'd say ninety percent. Shit. I had to go on Google just to get a damn date. Ya feel me."

"Trust me. I know."

"I know you do. Brothas like you sittin' up here with five and six women. If I was on my game I'd put all them cows out to pasture and scoop your pretty ass up like a double scoop of Rocky Road ice cream and make you a one woman man but you caught me at a bad time. All I want to do right through here is get away. I need to get away from men. My life has gotten to be so hectic. I just need some quiet solitude. But let me give you my card. Who knows how I'll feel tomorrow."

"I hear you. But I really don't think that's going to happen here. You know the good reverend and I go way back so when he suggested I come along to help attract folks I couldn't say no but I could certainly use some peace and quiet."

"So, tell me K.--outside of the obvious--what is it that has these chickens cluckin'?"

Knowledge smiled slightly.

"Not sure what you mean Ms. Love."

"You know exactly what I mean. I saw the crowd you had gathered around you. I couldn't really see you because they had you surrounded but I was just waiting for the secret service to run up and out to throw up a hand and say 'I love you North Carolina'. I just knew it was Obama."

Knowledge smiled again.

"Sorry to let you down but it's just me Ms. Love."

"So, why all the hoopla? Only famous people get that kind of treatment."

"I wouldn't say all that now. Can I call you Butter?"

"Sure baby. I was wonderin' how long it was gonna take you to break with all the formalities. But anyway, what the hell did you to do to get all these church going heifer's panties in a bunch? Shit. If it's that damn good I may have to get me a place in line."

Knowledge dropped his head to his chest, smiled and in a vain attempt to maintain some degree of humility whispered.

"I'm an author and I guess a few of these ladies had the occasion to get a hold of a copy or two."

"Get the fuck outta here!" Butter shouted before covering her mouth. "Now that's something you don't see every day. A Black writer... Damn! Half the brothas I know can't read let alone write. And here you are walkin' 'round here all cool, calm and reserved like you just any ol' average brotha. Makes me feel kind of tingly just sittin' this close to somebody famous."

"Stop it Butter. I am by no means famous. I'm no different than any other brotha out here tryna eat and stay alive love."

"Oh but you are and you're far too modest. Let me ask you something personal if you don't mind."

"Sure. Go ahead ask."

"Alright. Tell me this sweetie. How many books have you written?"

"Well, I've written five so far but only two have been published so far."

"And how many have you so far if you don't mind me asking. If I'm getting too personal just let me know."

Knowledge smiled.

"You're fine."

"Well, then tell me. How many books have you sold so far?"

"I guess somewhere in the neighborhood of a quarter of a million."

"Get outta here! And you're trying to tell me you're not famous. Nigga please. Anytime anybody does anything and they put the word million in the same sentence you'd best believe they're kickin' it. No wonder all these old dried up spinsters are sweatin' you in bunches. They lookin' for a bright young brotha to kick start their old tired lives and then to find one with money to boot. Shit. You're like the key to King Tut's tomb. These bitches are seein' Beverly Hills 90210 and don't think they're not. No wonder they lined up competin' and pretendin they retreatin'. Ain't that a bitch," Butter laughed.

"Seriously though Butter I wouldn't consider myself in anyway famous."

"You might not but these golddiggin' bitches surely do."

And if on cue Butter stood up, turned around and faced the packed bus.

"Excuse me travelers!"

The good reverend held his breath expecting at the very least the very worst and breathed a deep sigh of relief when she addressed the crowd in a most congenial way.

'Friends I want you to help me solve a friendly debate my friend and I are having. In any case, my friend Knowledge is a writer who has sold a quarter of a million books. Does that qualify him for celebrity status are in layman's terms make him famous? That's my question. I believe it does but my very modest writer friend wants me to believe otherwise. What do you think?"

A chorus of absolutely(s) and fo' sho came from the women who'd surrounded him moments earlier. They'd obviously read the book but it was the Reverend Goode's booming baritone voice that ultimately took center stage.

"Well, I know of one book co-authored by a few good men that certainly made them both celebrities and famous. And I use it each and every week to attract a good many of you to church but it's been in print for more than a minute now and though it's a classic, some say a masterful piece of writing I can honestly say that it's been a minute since I've seen all the hoopla surrounding a book as I have seen with my friend Knowledge's last two books so I can honestly say that that I do believe that he has *officially* join the ranks of the famous through his writings."

Mrs. Goode who sat by her side in her customary position shook her head in agreement.

The stout, elderly man and his wife who sat across from the good reverend seemed uninterested and indifferent but when Butter addressed him specifically he was hardly at a loss for words. I believed they referred to him as Wisdom.

"That's a tougher question than you think friends and without being too damn derogatory or hating as you young folks say I have to mention the what the Reverend

Goode referred to when speaking of the bible and those who authored it. And what I believe contributes to a person performing a great work or becoming famous time. Now like I said I'm neither trying to be derogatory or to hate on the good brother especially when he's accomplished something that so few of us do and with a quarter of a million in sales he obviously knows his profession and knows it well but I equate greatness and fame with time. So, and unless the brother wrote a true classic like Langston or Ralph Ellison I can't say he's truly famous. At least not yet. You got folks out there like Lil Wayne and Kanye West out there selling millions but if I said they were famous and great most of you would look at me like I all the bricks weren't in the wagon. Great? Famous? In comparison to what? Duke Ellington, Billie Holiday, Coltrane? Lil Wayne and Kanye couldn't hold a candle to these musicians. But I'm sure Lil Wayne outsold all of them combined. So, sales don't necessarily equate with fame or greatness."

Knowledge understood fully and had had the same thoughts far too often but before he could utter a word Butter jumped in.

"I ain't even gonna say nothin' but I'll tell you this. I work with a variety of people every day. Mexicans, Africans, all kinds of people from every ethnic group and Black folks is the onliest ones alla da time hatin' on and killin' each other. It's a damn shame. Here we got a man on this bus traveling with us that has accomplished something special and unique and you talkin' 'bout what he's done ain't great. Nigga what has you done in yo' life? And you got the nerve to be called Wisdom. Nigga I got mo' wisdom in my left tit than you got in yo' whole body."

A silence took hold and out of the depths there arose a tiny voice.

"Well, Ms. Love I for one agree with you. I, for one think he's famous and relevant and I'm going to tell you what. Where I go to school there ain't a lot of young people my age reading. And they sho ain't reading Shakespeare and Chaucer and I for one think that's why school is a turn off for so many of us cause it ain't relative t what's going on so they can't relate.. But all of my friend all have read Mr. Knowledge's novels and we can't wait 'til Mr. Knowledge's next book comes out. It's like, well somebody may have said all those were great but in my hood Knowledge is just as good if not better cause he's dealing with our issues and the one's that most affect us in our neck of the hood. You know what I'm saying Ms. Love?"

"I do baby girl. And I think a lot of the women who came primarily because Knowledge was going to be here would also agree. In fact there's only one clown on this bus who doesn't agree besides my friend Knowledge who is far too modest to agree."

Just then a rather attractive well-dressed young woman of about thirty-five, sporting locks stood up.

"You know I don't know your name and I don't know what your connection is with the author. I don't know if you're his publicist, his agent or just on his tip. Me, I came on this trip at a friend's suggestion. My friend's call me Truth and I would like to think of myself as a political activist. That is I spend my every waking hour working on the betterment of my people. I am currently UNC in Chapel Hill pursuing my law degree so I can have more leverage when I fight on my folk's behalf.

And I'm really not too interested in this man's fame or greatness other than how it relates to Black folks. I do care about what he's writing and selling and the effects it's having on our community as a whole. Is it saying something, conveying a message so that it works towards the betterment of us as a people. And after reading both of his books I know this brotha ain't doing nothin' but propagating that same ol' bullshit that the man been selling us since slavery. He ain't no better than FOX news. He ain't doin' no more than propogatin' that same ol' bullshit myth that the white man been sellin' all you simple ass Black women since slavery. He been telling you that there ain't no good Black men out there. And that's bullshit. All of you happily married Black women on this bus can tell you that's a lie and I come from a family where my family and all my uncles have been strong Black men. So, that bullshit he's writing to all you Black women who can't find or don't have a man blaming the man is all bullshit. And it's not the reason you don't have a man. You're on a retreat. It may be time to do some introspection."

Butter was having a hard time trying to grasp Truth's words or message could only counter with these words.

"Well, I have to admit I haven't read Knowledge's books but is two hundred and fifty thousand people have responded in purchasing his books there must be something to say for the brotha and his writings."

"Huh uh sister. Don't be brainwashed by a nice face and a handsome face. You've been brainwashed. This is America sista. This is the same America that made you slaves and sold you everything from Furby's to Pet Rocks. And America was able to sell it to you because Americans, that would be you and I aren't the brightest stars in the sky."

"That's exactly was I was trying to convey to the young lady," Wisdom chimed in glad to have someone on his side.

"We just went though one of biggest *invented* gas shortages since the 1970's and when the rest of the world is downsizing and looking for a more economical, more efficient Smart car, we and I mean Black people are out here buying Lincoln Navigators, Cadillac Escalades and every other SUV and all terrain vehicles like we over in Afghanistan driving through the desert and across the desert."

A loud laugh arose from the back of the bus and even the homeless looking brother had a mind to speak up.

"I know that's right yo. You could sell Americans sand in the desert. They so damn gullible and stupid. I know probably know better than anyone here. I was a member of Junior Achievement as a kid and started a very unique and enterprising company. That business helped me to get a four year academic scholarship to the University of North Carolina Chapel Hill."

"Okay sweetie. And all that to say what?" Butter interrupted.

"Let the brotha finish Ms. Love. You've said your piece."

"I'm tryin' to see where the brothas goin' old man."

"I do believe if you'd let him finish we'll be able to tell."

Hopeless smiled at the old man in acknowledgement.

"Anyway, I had a four year academic scholarship which I accepted. I was an academic whiz kid entering college at sixteen and there wasn't a thing that Carolina could offer that I couldn't handle. I graduated third in my class. But the one thing Carolina didn't teach was critical thinking. I never thought about how McDonald's would advertise the McRib sandwich or Happy Meal for a $1.99

or maybe run a sale on chicken McNuggets. My friends and I would be the first in line. Perry Ellis or Aeropostale came out with a new line of clothes and we would be the first in line. We were brainwashed and I believe that's the point Truth was trying to make."

"I'm lost." Butter interrupted.

"Don't you see that's the point. Most of us are lost and that's what makes us so malleable, so gullible. Most of us are so ignorant and we've been transformed into mindless, materialistic, megalomaniacs that anything thrown our way we latch onto and digest without the least bit of thought or introspection.

The day I graduated it was Alize and orange juice and it seemed like every liquor store in Chapel was sold out. So, I wasn't the only one out there caught up in America's marketing ploy. For far too many of us looking for answers and seeking a little more than the dream of a good job and success it was boy or heroin. And for those of us that us who were down with the hip hop culture it Coogi jeans and crack cocaine targeted at urban America. It was targeted towards Blacks and marketed just like everything else America sells. And we're so caught up in the latest material things that a college education being the gateway to success we forgot to tell our kids.

You see America creates a false standard of success. It convinces us that we're all overweight and half a heartbeat away from obesity and the next thing we know we're all down at the local CVS or Rite Aid looking for an instant cure so we can look like the new Jill Scott or Jennifer Hudson. And people are actually dying from the combination of Red Bull and 5 Hour Energy drinks.

Me personally, I chose cocaine because it was for the chic in crowd and look at me. Six years later here I am retreating to see if I can't stop long enough to get a handle on this shit. I can't comment on my man's books or if it has any literary value because in all honesty I haven't had the opportunity to read them but I can say this. Be careful of what you what you inhale and before you do you'd better look at the reasons behind it. Everything that looks good and feels good ain't necessarily good for you. Much of what you've been exposed to is simply to make someone a fistful of dollars without your health or welfare in mind. Remember America is first and foremost a capitalistic country. It's all about keeping you ignorant so the man can stuff his pockets."

"Okay, I listened. I heard Mr. Crackman crying but I'm still not getting the point. What is your point my brother other than you got caught up in the game like every other weak assed, brotha on that shit?"

"Damn sista! You really didn't hear the brother did you?"

"I heard him. He's just like all the rest of these weak brothas out here that get caught up. That's why there ain't no brothas out here. My point precisely." Butter replied.

"No sista. Pump your brakes. You're listening but really not hearing. That's exactly what Hopeless is talking about."

"Exactly!" Wisdom said shaking his head in agreement.

"We walkin' round here thinkin' or better yet not thinkin' and swallowin' everything that's thrown our way. And that's just what happens to a lot of sisters out here that don't give pause to think and just do what feels good with no thought as to the long term affects it may have on them. Too many of our Black women don't think and ain't particularly discriminating when it comes to their lives. That's why we have so many single parent households where the female is out there working night and day to support her kids."

"Oh, now it's the woman's fault because y'all no good niggas won't support their children?" Butter replied.

"I didn't say that at all." Wisdom replied calmly. "What I am saying is that when a woman ends up two or three children by different men--if she even ends up with one and the daddy's not around or can't be found it automatically becomes the brothas fault. Black men ain't shit. In reality, the Black community has a lot of problems but rape isn't one of them so in essence and not saying that it's a woman's fault at all but we have to be a little discerning and a little more discriminating when checking the resume. Women are as much to blame; if not more than men for our current situation. I don't know how many times I've heard it said that it takes a village to raise a child and I know from experience that at the very minimum it takes at least two parents to have any amount of success in raising a child. Right now we have a culture where we have single mothers warehousing children. Sure. They feed them and clothe them but they can't nurture or really provide them with what they really need. And so you have a lost generation who have no idea of what is of value moralistically or otherwise. They call them the technological generation. I call them fools."

"What the hell are you talking about fat man?" Butter replied. "What does that have to do with whether the man's book makes him famous.

Truth interrupted.

"I think what Mr. Wisdom is trying to say and I don't know if I can say it any more plainly than he just did is that if we as women are too place blame it should be on ourselves and we need to stop scapegoating. The blame is not on the Black men as America would love to have us believe but on ourselves. We are the ones that spread our legs and welcome him in. Let me ask you a question honestly sistas. How many of you have children and the daddy's not in the household?"

Heads turned while others dropped.

"My point exactly. And if Knowledge wanted to share his bed tonight with any one of you or all of you he most likely could. The way some of you have been pushing up on him I'm pretty sure he could have his way with almost all of you. The fact that he's ignoring you only makes his allure that much greater. But y'all don't know shit about the brotha other than he wrote a couple of books. Now when your Black ass wakes up pregnant who you gonna blame? Think about it. I mean really think about it. But brotha man is smart.

He's writing that same ol' typical bullshit about how some brotha man dogged you and it's so much easier to be the victim than to take the responsibility for allowing these things to happen to you. You're the cause of the problem. In all of my thirty some odd years on God's green earth I ain't seen a Black man walkin' round here pregnant yet.

The Blackman is not the problem ladies. The man would like you to believe he is. You are. You're your own worst enemy but when someone like Knowledge feeds into the stereotype of Black men being no good, lazy, deadbeat dads, and the reason for our drug infested, crime ridden communities you run right out and spend your last twenty to reinforce the stereotype. He's the scapegoat and I give him no credit for perpetuating the myth. White loves to blame the Black man for America's problems like the high crime rate and portrays us all as drug lords killing each other and the cause of every problem he can possibly conceive but I ain't seen a Black man flying no planes or commandeering no ships bringing that shit in everyday."

"Truth be told," Hopeless shouted out.

"Amen sista," Wisdom concurred. "You ain't never lied."

"Just believe in telling the truth is all..."

Knowledge who had been quiet throughout most of the conversation interjected as if he were a judge waiting to hear the closing arguments.

"Funny thing but I agree with almost everything said with the exception of me propagatin' the myth the myth that Black men are worthless and have no inherent value and are worthless. If that's what you got from my writing I apologize. That was not my intention and I written about with the exception of one have been at the top of their professions. One was a stock broker. The other a marketing executive. Both are in love. One's married and neither are dead beat dads. In every story there has to be conflict and both are deep conflict and deep conflict with the women they love. Hell, my mother and father were married for fifty-three years and loved each dearly but you can best believe that time-to-time there was some disagreement which resulted in some conflict. That's just the nature of relationships --Black, white, yellow, whatever."

Butter leaned over and whispered in his ear.

"Mighta been some conflict with mom dukes and pops but me believe me baby there would never be any conflict between you and Butter Love daddy. The only thing you'd have to do is write and let Butter love you. And you do believe Butter can do that don't'cha baby. You don't need any of these lame ass, inexperienced church going women to bring out the best in you. We're about to step at this next rest stop. Let Butter give you a preview of things unseen yet unseen and show you what can be. I want to show you. I'm gonna give you more than you've ever had in terms of a woman, a partner or a lover. And I don't want you to say a word baby. It's on Butter baby.

Just want you to see what you've been missing. And all I want u to do when it's over is tell Butte that you're an equal opportunity employer and give me the opportunity to apply for the position."

Knowledge did his best to ignore the woman by his side grinning broadly at her bold proposition although he did consider the proposition before continuing.

"Trust me. I'm by no means discounting my achievements as a writer and no I don't believe I am propagating any stereotypical myth about my Black brothas. That would be a condemnation of myself as a Blackman saying I or my brothas are of no account. I and those of you who know me know I wouldn't do that. Still, I think we've spent far too much time on too trivial a subject." Knowledge laughed.

"Picture that. Me being famous, a celebrity. The idea alone tickles me."

"You're just being modest K.," The good reverend shouted.

"Not at all. I wish I had your capacity for modesty and humility, But in all sincerity I'm flattered that you consider my writing readable when I hardly do. My goal is to join the legions of the great writers and so I must agree with Wisdom in his assessment of greatness and truthfully I have a long way to go. But I thank y'all for your love and support Knowledge said before reclaiming his seat.

"Love supported by blind faith. What the fuck!"

"Young lady!" Reverend Goode said in a disdaining tone.

"Sorry reverend. I'm just so tired of ignorant niggas walking around with blinders on like so many helpless sheep."

Before Reverend Goode could respond Butter came to Knowledge's rescue. She had grown quite attached to the man who now shared her seat and was making sure he if know else knew it.

"Good God almighty sista. I'm thinking yo' mama could have just as easily named you Controversy. Ain't a single solitary subject come up that you ain't been contrary to. The man came as close to an explanation and apology for your perception of his writing as you can expect. Your perception is your reality and that's fine. But you have to learn agree to disagree. That's what they call compromise."

"You right. And don't get me wrong. I'm not contrary to everything sista. I just don't go through life oblivious and with blinders on. But most of these people on here are churchgoers and by their very nature they believe anything they hear. What did Karl Marx say? Religion is the opium of the masses. Church goers are by their very nature non-thinkers who would cling to dogma than to explore and question. In essence they would rather believe than to think."

"Ooh Girl you signifying now. When you attack a man's faith in Jesus you messin' with things that ain't to be played with." Butter said sitting down.

"Got to go with Ms. Love when it comes to religion and a man's faith. That's something that you don't question," Wisdom murmured.

"Wrong forum for that sista. My sole reason for being here is to strengthen my faith. I' here to begin to learn to believe in things seen and unseen. That strength in Jesus Christ and his teachings; in things seen and unseen. I' hoping his teachings which I have not personally witnessed will help lift me from the devil's clutch. And believe me sista the devil is this here narcotic that has control of my soul. Don't knock faith sista. I'm putting my life into strengthening my faith and resurrecting my soul. You feel me? Ain't nothin' wrong with blind faith or dogma as you put it. With faith there's hope and without hope only despair." Hopeless said matter-of-factly.

"Amen," A chorus chanted from throughout the bus.

"And you Innocence... What is faith to you?" Truth asked.

"To be honest with you, I never really thought about it but I know one thing. I wouldn't challenge my faith or anyone else's when it comes to their believing in our savior the Lord Jesus Christ," Innocence stated adamantly.

"And why is that? Is it because your parents told you that your every fear, your every trial and tribulation and ever unexplainable thing that happens in your life will be taken care of because you have faith? Is that what you've been taught?"

"Not sure I would put it in those terms ma'am but I suppose you're pretty much correct?" Innocence replied.

"No, she is not pretty much correct. She is absolutely correct. The good Lord is all-knowing and all-seeing. He not only protects us in our time of need. He blesses us. There is not a member of our congregation who would not attest to the goodness of the Lord." The good reverend was sweating with passion now and it was more than obvious that he was passionate and vehement but that didn't quell Truth.

"I applaud you reverend for your oh so passionate rebuttal but then I'd be lying if I said I didn't expect it but I did so believe that this was a religious retreat and they not only came out of blind faith but y'all came to ponder the countless mysteries and to have their faith tested and reinforced and have their faith strengthened so as to come to know the true meaning of why they believe it is what they believe. Isn't that the true meaning of a religious retreat reverend?"

The reverend wiped his brow which was now covered in sweat. All was quiet now except for the sound of the passing traffic and the steady hum of the bus engine.

"If you don't mind reverend I'd like to address the young lady's question if you don't mind," said Mrs. Goode, "since I along with my husband came up with this rather novel idea to get away from the humdrum monotony that is our daily lives. We thought it a good idea to step back and reflect on the many blessings God bestows us on a daily basis. Not only did I think this would be a good time to stop and give thanks and praise but I also thought it a good time to thank Him and to strengthen our faith and to show others who are lacking in faith the many advantages and necessity for believing in Him who we hold most high."

"I never said I was lacking in faith Sista Goode. I was simply playing the devil's advocate."

"May I please finish Truth."

"Yes, ma'am. But in order to begin I think it of the importance that you be clear of the issue that is being addressed. And there's no need to run roughshod over my thoughts and ideas just because they don't coincide with yours. I thought and was under the impression that this was an open forum in which we as non-believers, devout Christians, Muslims and whatever could come together to strengthen our commonalities instead of bickering over our differences."

"Perhaps if you would let me speak we might do just that. However, I do not believe that you or anyone else has the right to question my fellow churchgoer's faith and beliefs since you do not agree with what it is they believe."

"Well, it would be quite difficult to understand you or your religious beliefs or your faith if I couldn't question you and yours about it. As I stated previously I'm not one to eat and swallow everything tossed my way. Because I am inquisitive by my very nature I am always in constant search of both truth and meaning in my life so I have to ask. I don't think it or mean to be offensive in any way and neither should you since it is this that all of you have such strong faith in."

"Girl's got a point there," Knowledge chimed in. "Let me tell you this though Truth. Twenty, no, maybe thirty years ago, my life was in shambles. I'd go to bed with Joyce one night, wake up with Sharon the next morning. The following day I'd lie down with Juanita and wake up with Jasmine the next morning and a hangover that wouldn't quit. Every day it was a different woman. People would look at me and ask what the hell was wrong. All I'd say was it was the day after the night before and then I'd repeat the process. It took me a few years before I began reaching out for something more, something different. After awhile I couldn't get their names right or that bottle out of eyesight. And so like my man Hopeless I sought help. I was at the end of my rope. I'm talking desperate and a number of people, both friends and family told me I needed Jesus in my life. I wasn't so sure about that since I saw people warring and killing each other since the beginning of time over Christianity. I read about the plight of the Indians and Blacks in slavery being subjugated in the name of Jesus Christ. I watched Christian parents pull their children away and forbid their children to talk to me as church was dismissed. I was skeptical to say the least. Then one day it dawned on me that this wasn't Jesus. These weren't His teachings but man's distorted interpretations of the man. And when I discovered this I went searching and I mean in earnest.

But I still wasn't convinced. I ran across people who referred to themselves as 'born again' and I said to myself quite literally that's what I need. I need to be born again! Then they asked me if I was saved and I said to myself 'Hell no I ain't saved!' This liquor and women are going to kill me! Why the hell do you think I'm coming to you? I'm trying to get saved from myself but it was like trying to join the Masons or some secret organization. Whatever it was, it sho appeared that they had the keys to the pearly gates but like I said it was like they had turned it into some type of secret organization for members only and they weren't accepting any new members and especially a whore mongerin', alcoholic like me. But I was so damn persistent that after awhile they just said 'Oh hell, make him a member and give him a key so he'll leave us alone.'"

"Persistence overcomes resistance." Wisdom muttered.

"Exactly! I just said that to say that you must keep challenging the powers that be Truth until you get the answers you need."

"And I intend to do just that," Truth said smiling broadly.

"You just keep asking the hard questions." Knowledge reiterated.

"Oh, I intend to do just that. That's why I'm here. And it occurred to me that if a person believes as firmly as these good people here tend to believe then sharing their beliefs would seem the right proper thing to do. Almost like passing on the torch of eternal light to us poor heathens in the dark."

Hopeless grinned.

"You know listening to you makes my heart warm. In my situation I ain't taking no for an answer. I ain't coming to the keepers of the flame and eternal light to be told ain't no coloreds allowed. Baby like you need I need some answers, some direction, some hope. I need them now and as far as that good ol' boy network and that no admittance clause I ain't having it. A Christian don't rest on his laurels. A Christian's work is never done as long as the next man is out there thirsty and starving. I have questions and need answers." Hopeless said grinning a painful grin through clenched teeth.

"Reminds me of something from the bible when God the Father subjected his only begotten son to the devil sending him into the desert for forty days and forty nights. And even though Jesus was an ideal son by any father's son he couldn't help question his Father. He needed answers.

I can also recall the story of Job who was an equally ideal servant. Yet, being ideal he hadn't been tested. It's easy to be good if you stay secluded and haven't been tested. The true test came when the Lord took him to task at put before him some dubious trials and tribulations to test his faith. But Job refused to question the Lord. I guess I am a little like Job. I don't have the gumption to question the Lord's motives but like Truth, Knowledge and Hopeless I will question you his followers for some insight. I figure if this life is my cross to bear and y'all know the secret to pass unscathed y'all sure as hell gonna give me the ammunition to fend off evil and like Knowledge said give me the strength and knowledge to be born again. And I know that as good Christians as y'all claim to be y'all ain't gonna just turn y'alls back on helping a poor wretched soul that's cryin' out for help."

At this point, one of the elders in the church got up from her seat, walked to the back of the bus followed by the good reverend placed her arm around Hopeless and hugged him as if he were her own son followed by the reverend's heartfelt embrace.

"We are only as strong as our weakest link," the good reverend said. "And with the Lord's help we will have you back on your feet in no time."

Seeing this, Butter who had quiet for longer than she had in her entire life squeezed Knowledge's arm and wiped a tear away smearing her mascara even worse than it already was.

"I really believe they gonna try and help that boy get offa that shit," Butter whispered to Knowledge.

"They pulled me through," Knowledge replied.

"I hear ya but they tell me it's harder to kick than alcohol, crack, or anything out there. And I swear fo' God it was hell when I was tryin' to kick."

"It all depends on how bad you want it. If you truly want it bad enough you can kick anything."

"That's so true K. It so depends on how badly you want something. You can have anything, anything at all if you really want it. Now tell me K. How badly do you want Butter love?" Butter said smiling before grabbing his hand and sliding it under her dress until he felt her warm moist mound.

Quite taken back K. tried to free himself from her grasp. Butter held tightly, leaning over to buffer others from viewing. And then with all her strength shoved two of his fingers into her vagina, gasped and began to rotate her hips on his fingers. He immediately pulled back only to find her grasp on his arm was even stronger than he could have ever imagined. Amused at the embarrassed scowl on Knowledge's face she laughed.

"Betcha you ain't never met nobody like Butter Love have you baby?"

All eyes were still focused on Hopeless who was now in tears. They had all given him their word promising through their own testimonies that they would do everything to help him to come to know the Lord Jesus Christ as they had come to know Him. And through them Jesus would rid them of his demons. Even Innocence sheltered from the ills of poverty, drugs and the scourge of growing up just blocks from the hood for most of her life and who'd looked condescendingly at most of the travelers was caught up in emotion. Extending a hand to the poverty stricken Hopeless who she'd looked upon with a disdainful eye only hours ago Innocence promised her help and assistance when the retreat was over handing him a neatly folded paper containing her number. The heartfelt gestures moved Hopeless to no end and it was the first time in a great many years that Hopeless felt like a chance truly awaited him. The tears flowed freely now. Tears that flowed like so many streams into all the rivers of pain and heartache he'd caused himself and countless others who loved him deeply.

"The worst thing in life young man is wasted potential but only a wise man can right his own ship and navigate it to calmer waters and dry land before it capsizes and lays waste to its crew. So, don't you condemn yourself for entering the murky depths of despair on this perilous journey. Life itself, by its very nature is never smooth sailing. Instead congratulate yourself for having the wherewithal to see calmer seas and brighter days just over the horizon," Wisdom whispered into the young man's ear. "In fact, I congratulate you. Some men never see the light and are dragged away with the undertow never to be heard from again."

Knowledge had a mind to go back and give his support to Hopeless if for no other reason than to get away from Butter. He knew he could be more of a help having gone through his own addiction but he knew when all the wishers were gone and Hopeless really needed someone he would be there.

"Can't bear to leave Butter can you?"

Knowledge smiled. Nothing could be further from the truth but he refrained from responding.

"Can I ask you a question K.?"

"It's never stopped you before," he said a light grin now etched at the corners of his mouth.

"See that there is why I like you boo. Here I just met you no more than a couple hours ago and you say shit to me like you've known me for years. I don't know too many motherfuckers I'd just let say any ol' kinda shit to me. Like that bitch Truth. She said a couple of things 'bout you that made me want to drag that lil dreadlocked bitch off this here bus and beat a damn perm into her ass. If I didn't have respect for you and some of these churchgoing sons of bitches, I'd wear her little militant ass out. But anyway back to you K. I'm a lil curious about somethin'."

"Go ahead love."

"Well, I may not be no rocket scientist or the brightest star in the sky. I ain't got no masters or PHD, ain't really one for all that book smarts but I can read most niggas. I have to you know. It's a necessary integral part of my job. My very survival depends on it. Ain't no room for error in my profession so whereas I may not be all that classy and hi-falutin'. I can recognize things most women can't see. I avoid the pitfalls. And it's easy to see that you're hundred percent Grade A beef. And a damn fine specimen at that. Ain't no sugar in your blood whatsoever. No suh... And yet you ain't got a bit more interest in many in any of them ho's tryna to throw the pussy at you than a man on the moon. Shit like that puzzles the hell out of me. A typical nigga woulda tried to play the hell out all of 'em. They lookin' all good and got all the book smarts in the world and here you is sittin' here wit' me who ain't got shit to offer somebody like you wit' all your education and book smarts. I ain't sayin' that I ain't got nothin' to offer or bring to the party 'cause I'm pretty damn sho' them heifers can't give you what I can but as far as being diamonds, they can probably outshine me in the daylight. Now after dark that's a different story.

But I just don't understand why you ain't doin' somersaults when they all but throwin' the poo poo at you. Instead you act like they don't even exist."

Knowledge turned to Butter and smiled.

"Do you believe in the notion that everyone has a soul mate, that one special person?"

"I never really thought about it."

Butter waited for Knowledge to go on but he was lost in deep thought now almost as if his own question had taken him somewhere faraway. Butter sat back now content with her

"You know I useta always fantasize about being rich and famous, having a big fine house, a big shiny new car with a driver to chauffeur me around, another to cook for me, one to do the gardening, one to lay out my clothes each day, you know--shit like that. I'd have a man for every occasion. And I'd have one just to love me down real good whenever I'd get an itch. You feel me?"

"You just don't know how much. I hear you and I feel you. I useta think like that. And I'll tell you all those things are nice. Had 'em all at one time or another and don't get me wrong enjoyed the hell out of it at the time. But like everything else it had its time and place. Now let me ask you a question love."

"Sure anything. I knew it was only a matter of time before you got tired of me grilling your ass and flipped the script on my ass. Be gentle though. Believe it or not I am kinda fragile."

"Relax. It's nothing intense. I ain't tryna put you on front street or nothin' like that."

Butter breathed an easy sigh.

"Whew! Well, that's a relief," she replied laughing nervously.

"I'm just curious as to your age is all."

"That's it? Damn! Here I am bracing myself thinkin' you ready to go for the jugular and tear my heart out and all you want to know is how old I am. Damn K. You sure are different than all the men I come across. I thought you was gonna ask me if I ever had a venereal disease or some shit like that. I guess that's why I find myself so attracted to you. But you know you sure as shit didn't have to go through all that just to ask me how old I was," Butter said relieved and smiling.

"Well, a lot of women don't like to be asked about their age. Their offended when men question them about their age."

"Oh, please! K. you should know that I ain't like that. We been on this bus for more than two hours. You should know me better than that. Anyway, I'm twenty-nine. And don't you say a word. I know I've got a lot more road behind me than most twenty nine year olds. Hell! How they say it? I been around the block so many times they could name the street after me. But I feel good. Why made you ask me that anyway?"

"No particular reason. I was just doing a little reminiscing. You know I can remember when I was twenty-nine. I thought I needed all of those things you mentioned to make me happy, to make me think I was living. I needed the cars, the women and I stayed up in the sauce. Wore me out. Damn near killed me. I'm not sure what I was looking for but I kept pushing the envelope. Don't know if I was thrill seeking and living on the edge or was simply trying to defy death. And I'm not exactly sure what motivated me but one day I was in a hotel room with this fine sista and we were kickin it. You know we had a couple drinks, smoke some trees and then we kicked it a couple more times. She was screamin' and yellin' and tellin' me how damn good I am and I'm feelin' good down to my toes cause she was one fine hammer and for her to tell me this made me really think I was the shit. And then she killed it. Getting dressed she made the about how she only slept with famous people and it suddenly dawned on me that I wasn't fucking anybody. I was getting fucked. And then my health started failing not long after. But I didn't stop there.

I flew down to Texas to see this chick who arranged a book signing for me where I spent the weekend in some hotel outside of Austin. This was right after Katrina and she was one the people displaced and she got a little money from her house which was destroyed and she was intent on keeping me there. Took me to New Orleans and showed me around and made sure she had every kind of liquor conceivable in that hotel room when we got back to Austin. And since the liquor was free and the pussy too I made sure that I had my fill of both. Those three days damned near killed me. I went straight to the doctor upon my return home and found that my sugar level was sky high. I had contracted diabetes and high blood pressure on that last trip and trust me that was my last trip up til now. Between the liquor, the women and the stress I was committing suicide.

I was dying of overconsumption. It was all a bit too much of everything. Not only was shit getting too thick I'd somehow gotten involved in four or five relationships and where I used to be at the top of my game I wasn't handling those either. So, what I did was pump the brakes. I had to. I took some time to sit back and made some hard choices and started thinking about my life and what it had become. And then I asked myself if I wanted to continue on this path to nowhere and realized that there wasn't much future in it. I figured out what I was missing; what was driving me and made a conscious choice to meet the demons driving me head on but for now I simply became celibate, started eating and exercising on a regular basis and began to know and understand who I was. Now it's a far simpler life. I rededicated myself to my children and my craft and even though I miss a good many things about all the women, the traveling and the partying I really and truly believe that this way of life at this juncture of my life suits me better.

Trust me though. That was only a couple of years ago so I'm still adjusting but for the most part I think I have a pretty fair handle on who I am and where it is that I want to go. I guess that's why a short skirt and a nice set of tata's don't really affect me the way they would most brothas. Guess I just had my fill. And you will too my love."

"And what about your demons?"

"What about them?"

"Do you still carry them around? Do they still haunt you?"

"Every day of my life and that's why I'm here today. It's come time to meet them and confront them head on one last time."

"You care to share?"

"That's one I can't but I will tell you this and I'm not one that usually gives advice. But if I had to share one piece of advice that I've learned it would be to let them name the block after someone else," Knowledge said staring into Butter's hard brown eyes. There was no pretense of a smile this time.

Butter lowered her gaze.

"I hear you. That's why I'm here. I'm tired. Tired of men pawing all over me when they have nothing better to do. I mean you can't beat the money but I'm tired as hell. I just needed a moment to stop and think, maybe consider a career change. I'm still fairly young ya know."

"Fairly young?" Knowledge laughed.

The bus was pulling into a truck stop and was apparent the riders welcomed the chance to get out and stretch their legs but none more than Innocence who finally had a purpose. Grabbing Hopeless hand she pulled him towards the front door of the bus only stopping briefly to address the good reverend and to pick up a small toiletry bag.

Wisdom followed making his way up the aisle just in time to hear the conversation between Butter and Knowledge.

"If you don't mind me saying so Ms. Love but I'm sixty-three years old and everyday that the good Lord endows me with breath I thank Him and say this is the first day of the rest of my life. My intentions are only to make that particular day better than those that have passed."

"I hear you good brother. She made me laugh though when she referred to herself as 'fairly young'. If she's fairly young what's that make us?"

"Ancient," Wisdom said smiling.

"Historic if you ask me."

"You know I've never really studied much and in no way am I in a position to really give advice but you do remind me of my own daughter for the world. Let me see.

Diamond's twenty nine and the girl's spent most of her young life trying to break down walls and barriers. Trying to get ahead she lets the world define her success. She's a beautiful girl and I guess that's why you remind me of her so much but I overheard you and it just seems to me that you both have one thing in common. And I'm not criticizing but you're both killing yourselves chasing something that's fleeting and has little substance in the overall scheme of things. Both of you are chasing the dollar. And if you just take a minute you'll find that a lot of men who never stopped to take pause have gone crazy chasing the same dream. So, I have the same advice to you that I give my daughter. Read. Read about the history of man and you'll find that everything you're going through has already been traversed. Now I'm not going to pretend that I know what kind of work you do but I can almost guarantee that it's already been done."

Knowledge couldn't help but smile.

"And not only has it already been done but if it's been done then someone chronicled it. Still, if it's not in the helping profession like a doctor or teacher and your simply working for the money you're going to come up empty even if you do amass some wealth. You see Ms. Love when you get to be my age you're going to find that money does not equate with happiness. But if you read and do a little research you'll find that you're not the only one that's been through this and that most everything you're doing and going through has been done before so like I tell my daughter don't waste your time trying to remake the wheel. It's already been made. There's a blueprint out there for everything. Even happiness but it's not money."

The old man made no inclination that he knew what Butter's occupation was but Knowledge was sure he knew. Hell, he would have been surprised if anyone on the bus hadn't guessed it by now but Wisdom wasn't necessarily concerned about the woman's occupation. He knew that the root of all evil and the driving force behind it all was money.

"Hope you didn't mind an old man putting his two cents in where it didn't necessarily belong. I just overheard you two talking and it struck me as funny that I had the same conversation with my daughter earlier this week is all."

"No sir. That's why I'm here. I'm looking to get a new perspective on something that's gotten old quick."

The old man smiled.

"Sounds like my life," he said just glad to have been of help. "Just didn't want it to sound like I was an old man being meddlesome."

"Hardly. I was just telling her the same thing although I'm sure I wasn't quite as eloquent as you my friend." Knowledge said grateful the old man appeared when he did.

The driver, a quite congenial balding white gentleman who had smiled the entire three hour drive as he listened now pulled into a lone of buses waiting for a parking space in the area designated 'Buses Only'.

"Okay folks. You can disembark just as soon as we get a parking space. It's one thirty by my clock and we'll be leaving at two o'clock sharp. Remember your bus number. It's one sixty four. Don't want you all ending up in Kalamazoo or some other God forgotten place." He said grabbing his thermos and helping the travelers off the bus.

The old man stood in the long line waiting to disembark. He stared at Butter who so reminded him of his daughter. She seemed to be lost in deep thought. Seeing her in this light Knowledge knew that she too was questioning her life choices. Patting her on her knee and remarked, 'Everything will be fine. Just give it some time, some thought and ask Him for some direction and it'll work itself out."

"I certainly hope so," Truth replied contritely. "It's hard to build a nation when we've got the likes of you destroying it."

Butter, used to this was suddenly aware of the young woman's presence and was immediately on the defensive.

"Who in the hell are you talking to trick?"

"Only trick on here is you and I hardly think I stuttered. I heard somebody say that if you don't stand for something you'll fall for anything. But hell if it's not bad enough that you don't stand for anything you don't just fall for anything but your ass will lay down for anybody. You're some role model for our young ladies. Ho's like you disgust me."

Butter was out of her seat now reaching, trying to get a handful of Truth but Knowledge grabbed her holding her firmly within his grasp. He had everything he could do to restrain her.

Why you little bitch I'll beat your rusty little nappy headed Rasta pretendin' Jamaican ass. The only reason ya'll come up here cause you ain't got shit there. And then you come here thinkin' you better than somebody. Ya'll so damn poor it takes one of you to go to the bathroom before the next one a ya'll can eat."

Snickers could be heard throughout the bus.

"We may be poor but we're rich in spirit. You sure as hell won't find my Jamaican sistas who gonna spread their legs and sell their souls for no stranger. Who does that?"

"Bitch. Has you got a man?"

"Yeah, I got a man. So what?"

"And how many ho's you been to get him to say he 's your man? Nigga take you to dinner and then the movies then get you home and spread your skinny red ass across the bed and fuck the shit outta you and all for under forty dollars. Now think about it bitch. Who's the real ho? Who's dependent on their man to pay the rent, put food on the table, and pay the electric? And what's the tradeoff for that? Every last one of us prostitutes ourselves for something so you be mighty careful who you callin' a ho, bitch. If anybody's a ho baby, it's you. If you was smart enough to have a job you'd go to work and do your nine-to-five where the white man pimps you an gives you an hourly stipend cause it ain't no fair wage and I guarantee he ain't paying you near what you're worth. He's pimpin' you you dumbass. He's usin' you. He's givin' you just enough to feed your kid. You workin' week-to-week and livin' day-to-day. What the fuck is that? You prostitutin' yourself for the man and he's gettin' rich off yo' ass and don't give a fuck about yo' ass. He's fuckin' the shit outta you you stupid ho and you got the nerve to turn pass judgement on me. You still a slave fool."

Up until now the good reverend had chosen to ignore this tirade hoping and praying that it would play itself out. When it didn't he was forced to step in.

"Ladies. Ladies. This is a time of reflection. There is not one of us that is perfect but we walking in his shadow must seek to achieve perfection. If we fall short and we will we can still achieve excellence but we must not throw stones if we live in glass houses."

Butter now too livid to hear anything continued her tirade.

"On the way home you pass Lord & Taylor's. You starin' at them boots. You know the one's you been dreamin' about all winter then you pass the Mercedes showroom and see that cute little 320iC. You want it but you can't get it. All you can do is wish and window-shop. Yo' man promised you he was gonna get 'em for you but it's been a year and your dumbass is still waitin' because you ain't been wit' yo'self. You prostituted yo'self and didn't get market value. Now you stuck and mad wit' the world cause you unhappy wit' the situation you in. That's a lesson my mama taught as soon as I got my first period. She'd say ain't no nigga gonna buy the cow when he can get the milk free.

In my case, if I see something I want I ain't waitin' on no man or nobody else. I work for myself. I'm independent. And there is no ceiling for me. I ain't boxed in by no nine-to-five. I ain't no slave to the man. I'm freer than your narrow ass will ever be. I set my parameters. I know my worth and ain't no man or nobody else is going to set a value on me or devalue Butter. I know my worth and gonna set my price. I'm what you're trying to become baby girl. I'm a strong Black independent sista and whether you like how I gets mine or not the fact is I gets mine. You better wish but then again with them bargain basement looks your anorexic ass couldn't give that shit away."

Truth dropped her head.

"Ever since you've been on this bus you've been hatin' on someone. First it was K. then Wisdom, Hopeless, the good reverend and even Innocence. And that's okay. But you chose the wrong one this time bitch. I ain't no churchgoer and I will fuck you up. When anyone is as mean and critical of everyone as you are it usually means that there is something inherently wrong with you. Problem is you don't like yourself. And the only thing I can tell you is find out what's really making you miserable and work on alleviating it. Now the only thing you have to reflect on this weekend is what's really bothering you and the other thing is when I'm going to put this size nine foot up your ass cause if there's one thing that's a certainty it is that I am going to beat your skinny, little yalla ass just for stepping to me. Count on that shit baby girl."

As if on cue the bus pulled in and the doors opened relieving some of the tension in the air.

Truth exited the bus quietly. It was the first time since the ride started that she was quiet.

Knowledge still held a firm grip on Butter's wrists though not nearly as tight as before when he was doing his best to restrain her but feeling a little more a little more at ease now he relaxed his grip and smiled. And after the battering she'd given Truth what more could she do? Butter had said her piece and made her peace. She had never felt comfortable with the monikers bestowed on her and so had chosen to call herself a customer service representative and referred to what she did as simply being a dispenser of pleasure. She had never had any qualms about her profession. After all it was the oldest profession known to man and with more than six billion people in the world she knew she wasn't the only one indulging regardless of the motivation. That was for damn sure. The only difference between she and most was the fact that she got paid--up front--for pleasing people and there would be no whispering, no more snide remarks, no more sideways glances. No. What she did was out in the open just the way she liked it.

Innocence grabbed Hopeless' hand and led him off the bus. Lord knows he'd felt better. It'd been almost a day since he'd had his last hit and his jones was now coming down on him harder than it ever had and he didn't know if he had to shit or throw up but what he did know was that despite his wanting to kick he needed a hit. His stomach was doing somersaults.

"Motherfucker," he screamed as if he had Tourettes but it was no Tourettes. It was that damn shit telling him it was time.

"You okay?" Innocence asked watching the sweat pour off the young man's face.

"I've felt better. My jones is just kicking in is all," he said trying to mask the growing nauseousness.

"Sorry babe. But you're gonna have to go slow and walk me through this. I don't know much about drugs or what you're going through."

"And I pray to God you never will, sweetheart."

"Ain't no way in hell! You don't have to worry about that. I've seen too many of my friends get hooked messin' around with that shit."

Another step and Hopeless doubled over and began vomiting profusely. Innocence backed up letting Hopeless languish in his own misery. When he was finished, he stood up doing his best to regain his composure before wiping his mouth on the sleeve of his jacket and made his way over to Innocence. The stench caught Innocence off guard and she gagged from the smell.

"How do you feel?"

"Wish I could say I feel better but I'd be lying. That's just the first step. But I'll be fine."

"Yes, you will... Come on let's go inside and get you cleaned up."

Hopeless followed Innocence into the truck stop and then did as instructed and headed for the showers.

"It'll make you feel better."

"Sure as hell hope so. I feel like shit."

Once inside Innocence took the small donation she'd taken up without his noticing and proceeded and proceeded to purchase some clean underwear, some socks, a pair of no name jeans and a shirt. They weren't the best. There were no designer labels but they were clean and if he was anything like her she knew that new clothes always seemed to make her feel better. It always made her feel like she had a new lease on life. Innocence only hoped that he'd feel the same.

With baited breath she handed the clothes to the good reverend and asked that he take them in to Hopeless who had not as yet exited the shower.

"It's a kind act you're doing. May God bless you my child," Reverend Goode said winking at Innocence.

Innocence smiled before heading to the restaurant after leaving a message with the reverend for Hopeless to meet her there.

Moments later Hopeless appeared before her looking like new money. He grinned broadly. Clean shaven, his dreads took on a different tint and Innocence had to admit he did clean up well and she was suddenly not quite as comfortable as she had been with the homeless man who she had only moments earlier accompanied.

Hopeless slid into the booth across from her and smiled again. The gratitude obvious in his smile, he thanked her for the clothes over and over. His appreciation heartfelt made her feel warm inside.

Moments later the waitress appeared before her brandishing two bowls of vegetable soup and a grilled cheese sandwich for Hopeless.

"I know it's not much but it's bland and with your stomach in an uproar I was afraid to order you anything else."

"This is fine. I just hope I can get this down," he said, the smile all but gone now as he sipped the soup before him.

"Do you mind if I ask you something rather personal?"

"Sure," Hopeless replied nibbling at the sandwich rather gingerly as if the sandwich was going to bite back at any second.

His stomach still felt queasy and he was glad to hear her speak taking his mind off the sudden nauseousness he was feeling again.

"So, tell me something. What exactly is it you feel when you're getting high?"

It was a tough question. He wanted to be honest with her but didn't want to glamorize it or peak her curiosity in any way.

"Well, it's a little like having sex or better yet making love for the very first time. You're like damn it feels so good almost like nothing you've ever known or felt before. And all you want it to do is keep going and going. It's like that dream orgasm every woman seeks but can't seem to achieve. And yet no matter how much money you spend or how often you smoke after that initial hit you can never recreate that feeling again. It's frustrating but you keep trying to reach Nirvana. I don't know if the thrill is in the search or the journey. What I do know is that you suck and pull on that pipe with every breath you can muster but no matter how hard you suck you just can't seem to get there. It's really hard to explain. It's like you're traveling to some exotic land and though you don't quite get there the trip was still fucking great. 'Scuse my language... People used to ask me that very same question cause I guess it looked like I was stuck in euphoria and I used to tell them that it was better than sex and if there was a heaven then this had to be it. And you know for a long time I really believed that."

"And what changed your mind?"

"Well for one thing I do enjoy making love and as you probably know no one likes to run a race where there's no finish line. If I make love I want to finish with fireworks," Hopeless laughed.

"Most people I know refer to it as 'chasing the dragon' though I don't know why. But to me it's more like chasing rainbows. You can see them but you can't touch them, can't feel 'em and if there is a pot of gold at the end it's elusive. It's like a dream, an enigma that can't be captured or possessed. And the whole time you're trying to capture and possess it you're going broke chasing it. By the time you finally wake up and come to the realization that you're never going to capture that so-called pot of gold at the end of the rainbow you're so physically hooked that all you end up doing is feeding your habit just to stay normal. Then when you let it go you spend weeks of going through what I just went through. Being sick and throwing up and praying Jesus will help you through this hell and then cussing Him for allowing you to go through this hell. I don't know how much of it is psychological but if you were to ask me I'd have to say ninety per cent. I can wake up, look at something like a commercial on TV about some type of soap powder or baby wipes--you know--something totally unrelated and it'll remind me that it's time for my nine o'clock wake up."

"What's a nine o'clock wake up?"

"That's that first hit of the day that gets me rollin', crackin' and fienin' for the rest of the day. After that first hit, that wakeup call I'd spend the rest of the day schemin' and hustlin' trying to come up with enough to support my habit and no matter how much I made it was never enough. I could earn a hundred or five hundred in a day and it was never enough. I chased the dragon for close to six years and went through hell. I watched brothers, good strong brother be reduced to animals, stealing and robbing from each other, hitting each other in the head for a couple of dollars. I saw sistas, fine sistas, bright, beautiful sistas sellin themselves for crumbs, for a five dollar hit if there is such a thing."

"What do you mean selling themselves?" Innocence asked naively.

"Prostituting themselves," Hopeless said sipping his soup. "I saw all of this and knew it was no more than the devil in all his glory hard at work corrupting people's souls and I made a vow that I would never get caught up in the game where I'd sell my soul to the devil for that shit. And then I realized that that shit was just the devil working in disguise. It took me from my relatives, family and all those that loved me. It left me alone in a den of thieves and those of the worst sort; storybook characters you only read about; gangsters you only see in the movies.

I went to rehab but it didn't help. Then one day I just woke up. I was tired. I was tired of chasing the devil and staying one step away from a charge that could erase everything I'd worked so hard for. Six years and I'd never gotten involved or caught up in anything serious and that's when it came to me that there was someone watching over me, taking care of me and making sure that nothing serious happened to me. It was then that I knew that I was here existing but for the grace of God. Oh, I had some close calls and some minor scrapes. I had days when I'd wake up with tears in my eyes and go to sleep with a butcher knife promising to end it all and praying for God's help. I prayed he would give me the strength to end it all and release me from my demons.

I hated the person I'd become. I hated my life and the depths to which I'd fallen but most of all I hated myself. I cursed Him one minute and I praised Him the next. Then one day it just came to me. It was like a revelation. And I said God helps those that help themselves and it was at this point that I made up my mind that I had to give my life over to Him, to bow down and pay homage and to want Him more than I've ever wanted anything in my life. So here I am."

The good reverend found the two engrossed in deep conversation and though he felt responsible for his flock he was glad the two loners had struck up a friendship. This was two less he had to worry about.

"Bus leaves in five," he said matter-of-factly.

"Perfect timing," Hopeless said smiling meekly and hoping he hadn't ignited her curiosity.

"Omg! I swear. I never dreamed," Innocence muttered just loud enough for Hopeless to overhear.

"I guess you wouldn't. Nice middle-class girl like yourself... I wouldn't expect you'd know anything about the people across the tracks. I am the people your parents warned you about," he laughed. "Come on before we miss the bus."

Innocence grabbed his arm.

"Why you little arrogant bastard!" she yelled. "Here you are walkin around lookin' helpless and homeless. And here I am trying to lend you a hand when the rest of the world has already turned its back on you and the minute you get a shower and some new clothes you wanna turn on the only person in your corner and insult her. And just to set the record straight, you don't know where or how I grew up Mr. Man."

The young woman who'd taken this vagrant under her care was seething now and content to let Hopeless have a piece of her mind in the middle of the parking lot.

Two elderly church members gathered not far from Innocence and Hopeless stood gaping.

"What happened Sister Willa?"

"Don't rightly know. I saw them walk in together. The girl was helping that boy in the rest stop."

"Can't be sure but from what I can tell I believe that homeless man tried to steal her bag. And after she was good enough to take up a collection for him too."

"Probably stole them clothes too. He sho' didn't walk in there with them clothes."

"Lord. Lord. Lord. I don't know what the world's coming to these days. You just can't trust nobody."

"Who you tellin' Sista Bertha," the two old women said before turning and walking am-in-arm towards the waiting bus.

Innocence was hardly finished and continued her tirade.

"Yeah, I live in a middle class neighborhood. And it's Black. And for the most part the folks that live there are hard working and do their best to provide for their children so they don't have to grow up among drugs and squalor and all the shit you think defines you as Black. I don't know where Blacks get the idea that if you don't grow up in the ghetto you're not really Black. What the fuck is that? Ain't nobody want to grow up in no shit like that. Who the hell in their right mind would want to subject their kids to that shit if they had a choice? Give half of 'em a chance to have a nice home in a safe neighborhood and all but the dumb and ignorant would be gone. But simple ass niggas like you walkin' round here feelin' like you ain't one hundred percent Black because you don't know what struggle is so you tryna immerse yourself in the struggle after your mama and daddy and their mama and grandfather done struggled so your dumbass wouldn't have to suffer through what they did. And your dumbass thinks he has to go wallow in the shit to say he knows what it's like to be Black and struggle. You's a dumbass. Walkin' round here like some wannabe hood that got caught up. You're nothin' but a trick that got fucked and turned out.

None of the brothas over there that have a half a brain and any amount of sense get caught up. Even the dope boys are smart enough to stay clear of that shit. What did Biggie say? You don't get high off your own supply. But not you Mr. College Boy. No, you're so insecure about what it means to be a strong Black man that you go the dregs of our community to see how grimy and gully you can get as if that's what it takes to be Black. Let me ask you this. In your twisted way of thinking do you feel any Blacker now that you have a drug habit? And if we so wrong for growing up middle class and wanting better for our children why have you chosen to ride with us and join us now as a last resort? Why the fuck you turn to us who ain't really Black for your redemption man?"

Hopeless dropped his head as Knowledge and Butter and a host of others looked on.

"This is shaping up to be quite a retreat," Sista Willa muttered.

"You ain't neva lied sista. And we ain't even there yet. I'm stickin' close to Ms. Love myself. I believe she gonna keep her word and beat that lil Jamaican gals ass."

"Lord knows you in mo' need of da good Lord Jesus than anyone here Sista Bertha."

"Go to hell Willa. I probably will hangin' around the likes of you. You just save me a cool place cause you'll already be there."

"Look at that. I can't believe Reverend Goode's gonna let that purse snatcher back on the bus."

"Now don't go jumpin' the gun Willa. You don't know that that boy did anything of the such. He looks like a good boy that just fell on some hard times if you ask me. Kinda cute too. Wouldn't mind a taste of that if I was ten years younger."

"Well, I've got my purse in the overhead compartment but I've got all my money right here," she said patting her breasts.

Hopeless was more than a little embarrassed as he made his way up the steps and onto the bus. His only relief came with Reverend Goode's announcement asking everyone to change seats so as to get to better know each other. Still, he hadn't come to make enemies or alienate folks and especially Innocence who had been more than kind to him. Aside from that she was just as cute as she could be. And Lord knows she was certainly a welcome relief, a breath of fresh air after spending so much time with the dregs of the earth.

He wasn't exactly sure how he'd offended her but whatever he said didn't warrant losing the only friend he had in the world. And now with Reverend Goode's latest announcement he wouldn't even have the chance to make amends. Still, he had to at least try.

Noticing she hadn't followed the good reverend's suggestions and was still sitting alone in the spot she was prior to the rest stop, Hopeless approached her tentatively.

"I'm sorry if I offended you Innocence. You mind if I sit next to you?"

"And why would you wanna d that? I'm sure you can find someone a little closer to your liking, a little closer to your neck of the woods, a little more ghetto and a little closer to your comfort level."

At least she wasn't yelling at him now but the words still stung. Still angry she had at least regained her composure.

"Believe me baby girl I am truly sorry. Sometimes I tend to be a little too arrogant and a bit too egotistical but you've got to believe me. You're the last person in the world I'd want to offend. It would mean the world to me if you'd forgive me."

"Sit your dumb ass down Hopeless." Innocence said gazing out the window.

Truth who had grown quiet following her confrontation with Butter found a seat next to the good reverend's wife. Both women exchanged pleasantries and it was the good reverend's wife who spoke first.

"Can I ask you a question sweetheart?"

"Sure, Ms. Goode," Truth replied cordially. Butter's words still rang in her head and she had to admit they bothered her. The last thing she would have considered coming on a religious retreat was some ho promising to beat her ass. And even though she fought for the cause each and every day she had never been one for physical confrontations. And Butter had made it clear that she was going to beat her ass. She was scared.

"Well, aside from seeming nosy I'd like to know why you're so angry."

Truth weighed the question heavily before replying.

"I'm far from angry, Ms. Goode. I just try to stay abreast--you know-- socially conscious is all," the young woman said trying to wrap her quivering lips around a smile. She had been shaken by Butter and the affects could still be seen. She had now made it a point to avoid any further controversy for the remainder of the retreat but now here was the reverend's wife with her holier than thou self provoking her again. This was the same Ms. Goode who had seemed so serene, reserved and withdrawn that Truth had at first labeled her a trophy wife worth no more than lying down and preparing meals for the good reverend.

Now here she was questioning her without any worthwhile pretense.

"Well being socially conscious is always a good thing but being so without assuming others are as well can present a problem of sorts. Often times you give your audience or those you are in discussion with no credit for having a varied opinion. Often times when people are trying to achieve a goal there are various ways to get there. There is no right way or wrong way there is only the way that is most convenient and comfortable to that person. Take Malcolm and Martin for example. They both had one thing in common. They loved Black people. They wanted to see progress and change. But and even though they had a common goal they differed radically in the approach. And you know what? Both were wildly successful in their own approach though they differed greatly in their approach and strategy.

Other times the way in which it's presented poses a problem of sorts. And the way it which you present can and is viewed as a personal attack. And I fear that's the way some of the churchgoers took you. And I'm not saying you weren't right in many instances. It's just the way in which you presented your argument."

"I hear you Ms. Goode but the Black race is in a sorry state of affairs and for far too long we've been sugarcoating our plight and our collective problems and instead of moving forward we're taking baby steps while the rest f the world leap frogs over us like we're standing still."

"This may be true in a great many instances and I have to agree in large part with the problems that affect us as a people but I'm sure you'd agree with the old adage that you can attract more bees with honey dear."

"I agree but there comes a time when we have to stop pussyfootin'--excuse my language--with those so-called brothers and sistas who are draggin' all the achievements and all the triumphs we've fought for and suffered since our arrival on this continent. They're pullin' us down with their irresponsible and reckless actions. And I'm sure you know exactly who and what I'm talkin' about. I'm talkin' about all the little dope boys runnin' round scratchin' each other's eyes out for a couple of dollars. I'm talkin' about the all of the idiot rappers who sensationalize the drug game and killing each other. I'm talkin' about all the sistas on public assistance who keep churnin' out babies to keep those government checks comin' in without a clue as to how raise and nurture a child then tellin' daughters on the way down to Sally's Beauty World that all you need is some purple weave and if you undress right you can get money and cars and be a trophy for some ghetto superstar if you do it right. I'm talkin' about the sorry ass brothers who run around the streets just like the masters did back in slavery promisin' these little lazy, shiftless, uneducated, love sick broads love. Then walkin' away and out of their lives once he impregnates them without so much as a 'see you later'. I must admit you sound almost Republican in your delivery and I guess that's where I have my problem. My problem is not so much what your sayin' but the way you come across. It's your delivery.

You know I took a similar approach when I was younger, much younger and then just by chance I came upon a very wise man who was my age chronologically but was much older and much more mature, and compassionate. I was attending Columbia at the time and was marching around campus protesting this and that, handing out leaflets and beating the war drums. I was beating all the doubters, nonbelievers and nonthnkers across the head with slogans and the idea of right in a world that seemed so wrong.

I knew. I just knew I not only had right but the Lord Jesus Christ on my side so there was no way I could be wrong but no matter how much I believed and professed to be right, no matter how obvious things appeared to be I wasn't getting my message across. And do you know why?"

Truth nodded before replying.

“I have no idea other than we are in a nation of ignorant, uninformed, miscreants.”

That’s true in part,” Ms. Goode replied, ‘But it’s so much more than that. First of all, let me tell you what this very wise told me. He told me never to place my values on others My values like my looks are something I had very little to do with. Both arise from other sources. In my case, they arise from my parents and took a lifetime to accrue. So, to be fair I cannot expect because I believe and can substantiate what I know to be factual to be adhered just because… So in turn what I am trying to impart to you young lady is the fact that Rome wasn't built in a day. So, I implore you to show patience when introducing new concepts such as your values to someone with the idea that you're bettering that person's quality of life. And last but probably most important is to be tactful with your delivery after all it is simply an introduction. If presented correctly with tact and patience they'll bite and come back for more. But never attempt to force feed them.

And then he taught me perhaps the greatest lesson of my young life and that it is to have patience. He said Melinda never force anything. *Every man finds his God in his own time.* That very wise man who I still refer to is now my husband, the Reverend Goode."

"So, what are you telling me? Not to say anything and just let things steamroll without addressing the ills in our community?"

"I'm not saying that all. What I am saying is to tone down your delivery. Practice tact and humility and you'll convert a lot more people than confronting and putting them on the defensive. Take your conversation with Knowledge. You had a captive audience and made some valid points until you attacked him personally. That's when you lost them. You let passion and anger overtake you."

Truth laughed heartily. The laughter rose from deep in her bosom.

"I guess you're right," she said still laughing.

"What's so funny," the good reverend's wife asked.

"Nothing really. Just that I heard one of the old ladies in the back say something similar when she didn't think I was listening tell her friend that I need to get me a man and get me some of that good ol' fashioned sex funky lovin' and I wouldn't be so mean and ornery is all."

Both women laughed.

"I must concur with sistas Willa and Bertha. It's always good to keep the plumbing in good working order. Releases tension and prevents stress and backup buildup." Ms. Goode added.

"It has been quite awhile," Truth laughed.

"I just know Reverend Goode didn't think I was going to give up the best seat in the house," Butter remarked to know one in particular. "And it don't look like you was tryna run too far yo'self," she said now referring to Knowledge while popping a piece of bubble gum with all the reckless abandon of a ten year old at recess.

"So, K. is you gonna let Butter be your mainstay when all this is over," she asked as she gathered her belongings around her.

"I'm not sure I know exactly what that means Butter."

"You right about that baby. You ain't gotta clue what Butter Love has in store for you."

Knowledge couldn't help but laugh. If nothing else the woman was comic relief although she was quite serious in her plans for him.

"Trust me baby. Butter knows what it takes to make a man feel like a man."

"I believe you baby," Knowledge acknowledged tying his best to cut her off before she started to elaborate but elaborate she did.

"You know when this retreat is over I'm getting out of the game. I pretty much knew that when I came. This retreat was no more than proper closure for me. But that still doesn't mean that Butter Love is through with men. In fact it means just the opposite. The only difference is instead of spreading the Butter around I'm going to concentrate my love all in one place. Can't let the skills fall to the waste. I've been told on countless occasions that I had a gift that I was blessed and my daddy useta always tell us that the worst thing in life is wasted potential. It's like giving God the finger when you throw away one of His blessings. No. When I came on this here little pilgrimage I was coming to give myself some time to think and choose a direction in which to proceed next. And I guess the good Lord was looking out for me. He put you right here in my life and Butter gonna make you her number one lover man, baby. Like I said before Butter gonna show a brotha how he's s'pozed to be treated, how he's s'pozed to be loved. And don't you worry baby all this is on me. I know the do's and don'ts, the when's and the won'ts and the difference between the two.

I know when a man feels the need to step up and be a man and when he wants his woman to take charge. I know because I've studied men. And even though yo highly intelligent and plus a gentleman don't make no difference. You human and still got needs and trust me Butter Love knows all about that. There gonna be days that you just wanna come home and fall into that easy chair. You useta bein' a bachelor so you don't wanna hear no mouth when you come in after a long hard day and haveta think about no wife, no kids or nothin'. That's when Butter steps to you and unties your tie takes that suit jacket off and removes your shirt before handing you a glass of Hennessey over ice. I'll give you a deep shoulder massage right up until that Hennessey takes over and then I'm out.

On other nights when I see that you're upbeat though still exhausted I may take more liberties and after I remove your shirt and tie I may drop to my knees and just nibble and suck on your dick like I's a banana smoothie on one of them one hundred degree July afternoons. And why? Because Butter's perceptive and knows just what her man needs at just that particular time.

On other days your tired ol' fifty one year old ass will come in the house feeling like you twenty five and want twist my wig and bend me over the kitchen counter in all of two minutes and two seconds just like the love connection. Well, Butter Love gotcha there too baby but don't get it twisted baby. It ain't gonna be none of that come in hit it and quit it. You gots to put your time in and work Butter. She likes to get hers too man. Knowledge gonna give it to her and make her feel like she's the best piece of ass he's ever had in his life. And don't worry there don't have to be no ties, no relationship, no nothing. I don't want you to feel like you bein' forced into nothin'. How that sound? Sound like a plan to you?"

Knowledge was more than a bit taken by the whole premise. In a little less than three hours she'd gone from perfect stranger to bodyguard and avenger to lover and mate. He had to smile. He'd known a lot of women in his fifty six years but none quite as forward or assuming as this woman called Butter Love. The sad part was that she was serious.

"Well whatcha think lover? I don't know too many men that would flinch or even hesitate at the proposition. Still, you ain't the run-of-the-mill sort of trick so I'm gonna let you sleep on it for awhile. But you know what they say. Think long think wrong."

Both the good reverend and the old man known as Wisdom overhead the woman's proposal and were shocked at her directness and the proposition itself.

"I must say it's an interesting thought," the good reverend commented careful not to say too much.

"That it is and it certainly beats any proposal I've ever had."

“I must say I’ve had some interesting ones but never had one quite like that,” the good reverend said. “Perhaps I shouldn’t say this as a man of the cloth but a few years ago I may have taken her up on that offer,” the good reverend smiled as he leaned back reminiscing.

“Good thoughts?” Wisdom asked sheepishly. He’d been a member of The United Christian Fellowship in God Almighty for close to ten years and had enjoyed the good reverend’s cutting edge sermons but aside from a simple greeting he’d never spoken to the reverend in any capacity other than the neighborly way. Reverend Goode had always intrigued him. He was a handsome man unlike himself and only seemed to get better looking as he got older. When there was a guest speaker at United soliciting or do missionary work for one good cause or another he would usually turn his focus to Ms. Goode. My god was she fine. She was unquestionably the best looking woman in the congregation and despite his fiery sermons they were both so reserved and cordial that and although it'd been ten years he knew as little about the reverend good now as he did when he'd first joined the church.

"Believe it or not I was a man before I ever became a man of the cloth and in those days I would have surely taken her up on her proposition. I'll tell you what Wisdom, I don't know if you know this or not but Knowledge and I go back to our freshman year in college. And I'll tell you what. We used to run them lil fillies up in Harlem. You couldn't have asked for a better place for two young brothas to attend college. Here we were in one of the finest colleges in the land with Harlem as our playground. I'm telling you New York had and still has some of the finest women in the world and Knowledge and I had our fair share that's for sure.

"At the time I was a divinity student but everyone thought I was a med student focusing on gynecology," the good reverend laughed as he recounted his college days.

"What brought you around?"

"Well, I gotta admit. I truly loved women."

"Guess that's most of us." Wisdom added not dare letting the good reverend off with some bullshit elementary explanation. "I mean for one reason or another most of us are attracted to the opposite sex. In fact, for far too many of us we are not only attracted to the opposite sex but for many of us, myself included it can become an almost incurable addiction. And being in the Big Apple and privy to some of the most beautiful women in the world after being raised in the backwoods of North Carolina. I'm just amazed at how you went there and didn't get caught up."

"Who said I didn't? Lord knows I loved women as much as the next man if not more and my first three years of college I stayed broke trying to love as many as I possibly could. Back then I thought I was the man. You couldn't tell me I wasn't God's gift to men. There was even the day I had the unenviable pleasure of sleeping with three different women and I don't mean at the same time. One was a close friend. One was my girl and the third was someone I had a newly acquired interest in. It wasn't something I'd planned and I never saw myself as a player or anything like that. I just loved women, always have."

"I don't think you're any different than most men. It's probably the biggest reasons I came along."

Wisdom's facial expression made it plain to the good reverend that the nature of this issue which had at first seemed lighthearted and jovial to both men was troubling the elderly man greatly and was hardly a laughing matter. The Reverend Goode noticed the sudden change in the old man's demure and was aware after having spent close to twenty years in the ministry that no amount of prodding would elicit what would be tantamount to an admission or confession on the old man's part. No when he was ready he would come forth but only in his time and of his own accord. Still, there was something about this man, a deep calm, a sense of self that intrigued the good reverend. He couldn't put his finger on it. He didn't know if it was the fact that the man ten years his senior who was both wise and introspective was inquiring of him an average man as if he could afford him something of an epiphany or revelation that could turn his life around. He didn't know if it was the fact that since he was a small boy he'd always respected the words of the elderly who he questioned endlessly for their wisdom and insight which he found limitless in his own quest for answers.

But this man who possessed more knowledge and understanding than most if not all the men he knew was prodding him, inquiring of him and it puzzled him greatly.

"May I ask why you're so intrigued by my previously life," the reverend heard himself ask.

Wisdom smiled a less tense smile this time before replying.

"Well reverend it's occurred to me that that all present or most of those here are here to confront or at the very least make peace with their demons. Hopeless, Butter and Knowledge have already come forward and made plain the afflictions which plague them and there's no doubt that a good many more will come forward as the weekend progresses. For some of us and depending how deep the issue depends on how readily we come forth. For some of us pride is the major obstruction and it's a sad thing because until we can overcome our pride we'll remain in the throes denial, beleaguered and unable to move forward," Wisdom said breathing a deep sigh of relief before continuing and the good reverend came to the sudden realization that this man with all the intellect of the other travelers combined was wrestling with demons far greater than he could ever have imagined.

"But you know I have never been a big supporter of the old adage that familiarity breeds contempt. Instead I choose to believe that familiarity brings a sense of comfort allowing one to empathize and in turn allowing one to share his most heartfelt afflictions. Your confessions make it just that much easier to share with you. And I come to you with mine because if you can, a man of the cloth, a learned man who I hold in the highest regard can divulge your trials and tribulations to me then perhaps I can finally put my sorrow and regret away and pick up the remnants of a broken man. I don't expect an answer to what plagues me. For only God can forgive the sin that I have committed but perhaps if you can lend an ear it will relieve me some of my anguish."

The good reverend smiled.

"Trust me brother I by no means mean to be judgmental and I pray that you don't deem me to be as such but if I had my druthers I'd make shame and embarrassment a cardinal sin. We are by our very nature human and prone to err in our humanness."

"I hear you reverend. My shame and embarrassment has held me back for far too long and left so many things that demanded my attention unresolved for far too long and certainly left my life in a state of chaos."

"Listen brother. We are all no more and no less works in progress. As much as we seek to achieve perfection in an imperfect world we cannot discount our humanness and that in and of itself does not allow us to be perfect."

"I hear you and agree with you wholeheartedly reverend. But I'm still waiting to hear how you curtailed your lascivious ways and came to be with your lovely wife."

"Well, to be perfectly honest, I never curtailed my lasciviousness. I chased and lusted after every skirt that came my way. At the same time my roommate, Knowledge had grown tired of the chase and fallen in love. She was a most attractive girl and smart as a whip. He met her as some activist rally they had on campus and it was obvious after the first time they laid eyes on each other that it was a match made in heaven. Not long afterwards they became engaged and from that moment on it was a wrap. No longer was he on the prowl and he began spending more and more time around the apartment as did she. And everything was cool. We became fast friends and I started to reassess my life. And although I saw what attracted Knowledge to this woman I never crossed the line. After all, there are boundaries. Knowledge and I'd been friends since grade school and the last thing I'd ever want to do was hurt him. In any case, she was several years my senior and much more mature than I was. And it seemed that every time she'd drop by the house I was entertaining someone different. And for some reason when I was in her presence I was always embarrassed by this and although we talked about everything under the sun she never ever brought up my womanizing even though I sensed that she didn't approve. Sometimes I wished she would. It was like; we talked about anything and everything under the sun. We'd have some very spirited, very heated discussions but never not once did the topic of my womanizing come up.

Then one day out of the clear blue, I guess curiosity got the best of her and she asked me why I dated so many women. And being that I didn't know myself I gave her some ol' cock-and-bull answer that each of them offered a little something different and together they made up a whole.

She smiled, seeing right through me and she made it quite plain that I was simply trying to fill a void and that as a divinity student I had the answer right in front of me if I'd only seek Him out. And I'll tell you, that woman's words put me on the right track and probably saved my life.

Not long after that she and Knowledge came to a parting of the ways and I grabbed her on the rebound and begged her to marry me. I didn't give either of them time to have proper closure. I knew it was wrong but I knew she was my soul mate, the element that would complete me and make me whole. I didn't give her a chance to think or to come up for air. She was devastated by the breakup and needed a friend to lean on and I was there to comfort her.

What I didn't know was how deeply I'd hurt my brother and best friend. It was years before Knowledge would speak to me. And I'm not sure if he's ever forgiven me."

"And that's your cross to bear?"

"I suppose it is. And every time I look at Melinda I wonder if I hadn't interfered if she wouldn't have been happier with Knowledge. I've had to live with it for the last twenty eight years and Lord knows I've prayed for forgiveness from both the Lord Jesus Christ and from Knowledge. And I still don't know what sins I've committed are the most grievous. I don't know if it's avarice or geed, the betrayal or simply the coveting another man's wife. But like you said I guess it's my cross to bear. But enough about me what's your cross to bear my good man?"

"Unlike yours reverend mine haunts me my every waking hour."

The elderly gentleman gazed down at his feet rather dejectedly.

"Come on good brother, the truth will set you free as they say."

"I confront the truth on a daily basis reverend. And I am hardly free." Wisdom stated but there was no humor in his tone.

"Let me tell you a story reverend. Thirty years ago I went to a small state college in western Pennsylvania where I met a most wonderful young lady prior to graduating and fell deeply in love. When I graduated I returned to New York which was home. I had the good fortune to find a teaching job not long ago after I got home.

My lady friend followed me to New York. She was several years younger than I was and though what we had in college had been more than enough when I returned to New York it just didn't seem enough anymore. Guess you and I were pretty similar in that respect. Everywhere I turned there were beautiful women. Black, Puerto Rican, Dominican… I was young, dumb and full of cum. Excuse my language reverend. But you get the gist. And it just seemed ludicrous that I be saddled with one woman when there were all these women at my beck and call. The funny thing was that I loved this woman. But I too was searching for something. I just didn't know what it was. What I thought I was searching for I found in the soft brown eyes, the full thick lips and the healthy chocolate thighs of every sweet young sister I ran across.

The fact that my college sweetheart had come this far to be with me once again was the best fit for me and for all intensive purposes a god send and the fact that she could be my soul mate never occurred to me. I was too young and dumb to realize so I continued to rip and run from borough-to-borough chasing skirts but I always made it a point to see her or she see me. I knew she was in love with me and I with her but I couldn't stop and settle down with the world at my fingertips.

At night I moonlighted as an armed guard out in Queens and one night I decided to surprise her and ran up to the Bronx to see her when I got off. I jimmied the lock when there was no answer at the door and walked in to find my baby in bed with another man. I shot him six times in the head before I had a second thought and did five years for manslaughter. That was twenty years ago but the thought of me taking another man's life is a thought that never goes away."

The good reverend had a career of hearing confessions but never had he considered this man so warm and of such calm reserve to be capable of taking another man's life. It took the reverend several minutes before he could manage a response.

"Did you ask the Lord for forgiveness?" was the best he could do.

"Every day," Wisdom whispered a tear trickling down his worn face.

"And you served your time? It's sad how events affect our lives but our God is a forgiving God. Do you know the story of the transformation of Saul to Paul?"

"I'm vaguely familiar with it."

"Do you mind if I tell you the story of Saul's transformation? I think it may lend a hand in your dilemma."

"Saul was a persecutor of Christians. God confronted Saul one day on the road to Damascus and asked him 'why do you persecute me'? When Saul couldn't give an answer God blinded Saul at which time Saul asked for forgiveness and changed his name to Paul and transformed himself giving his life over changing his name to Saul and promoting the Word of God. I think the most important thing about the story of Saul's transformation is that on that day Saul met God on the road to Damascus was the first day of the rest of Saul's life. With God's forgiveness Saul was able to start over. He was redeemed. He is a forgiving God and if you ask forgiveness then he will forgive you as well. Redeem yourself but don't live your life trying to undo something that can't be undone."

"I hear you reverend and I thank you," Wisdom said the tears flowing freely now.

"You've been carrying this burden for all these years. I think you owe it to yourself and the rest of us to come from behind the shadows and let the world see the transformation and what you have to offer the world. There is a position open for deacon you might want to think about. It's a chance to really immerse yourself in the Lord's work and grow closer to Him and get to know yourself better as well."

"I'll give it some considerable though and talk it over with the missus. Thanks for the offer and the words of encouragement reverend."

"And I thank you for listening Wisdom."

"What I've told you I've told you in the utmost confidence. I only hope that it will not go any further than you. Do I have your word reverend?"

"I promise you it will go further than me and my boss bears witness. But brother I believe you now have the answer to your dilemma."

The two men sat in silence for some time each wrestling with their own dilemma when two older church women approached the good reverend.

“Reverend Goode Sista Bertha and I have a bone to pick with you,” Sista Willa said pointing a skinny finger in the good reverend’s face. She was by no means happy.

“Reverend Goode we have been on this bus for close to three and a half hours now and we have watched you chit chat and mingle with everyone ‘cept me and Sista Bertha. You of all people should know that God don’t like ugly. And we feel like you been discriminatin’ against us the whole time we been here on this bus. Ain’t he Sista Bertha?”

“You ain’t neva lied Sista Willa. I believe they call that age discrimination. It’s a damn shame the way this here society treats its elderly. But you would never think right here in our own church we’d be subjected to that. And here we is—both of us—upstanding church members who ain’t never caused nobody no problems. And you rather concern yo'self with these here heathens than give us good Christian women's a lil time. It's a damn shame and here we done paid good money to support you and dis here church and this is the way you treat us."

"Tell him Sista Bertha. Shoot we may be a lil past our prime but we still got our needs and we likes to have a good lookin' man like yo'self pay us a lil attention. Hell, much as we paid for these got durn tickets that seems like the least you could do, reverend."

Wisdom who had been close to morose after his confession was now grinning like a rat in a cheese packing factory.

"No. He's got to do more than that. Good as you lookin' in that there suit the least you could is get up and model it for us. Now stand up and turn around so I can see the way it hugs that cute little butt of yours."

"Lord have mercy. No you didn't. Girl you is crazy. And with his wife right there…"

"What? I ain't tryna take nobody's husband. Just need a lil inspiration is all. Now stand up reverend so I can take your picture. May need to violate you a little later tonight... Now stand up reverend and pose for the camera."

Wisdom was now biting his lip to stop from laughing out loud. He was only too tickled to see the always composed reverend in unfamiliar straits.

"Don't know what you're grinning about," Sista Bertha said her sights now firmly set on Wisdom. "You ain't half bad yo'self and Sista Willa gonna need a weekend escort as well and you ain't never known lovin' until you done made love to a senior. Whatcha think Sista Willa?"

"Yeah. He's doable."

Wisdom grin vanished.

"Don't get your panties in a bunch gentlemen. I'm probably in better shape than most of the women aboard this here bus. Shoot. I walks everyday and I mean everyday just so I can be ready for times like these. Not only that I eats my turnips and add a stool softener as a daily supplement. And I don't just be out there givin' my stuff away like some common ho so it's good and tight just like when my mama birthed me. Am I lyin' Sista Willa?"

"Bertha ain't never lied," Sista Willa said shaking her head in agreement. "I's known the woman since we was damn near kids and I ain't never known her to nobody but once to them two twins when me and her went to the drive in back in '76. I went to the snack bar to get some popcorn and came back and she was doin' both of 'em. One was on top of her just a bouncin' up and down and the other had his…"

"Sista Willa don't you dare tell these young men about my black out. I swear one of them boys gave me a roofie."

"Roofie or no roofie Bertha, you was one happy sista. Ain't no way them twins coulda got your big behind into that backseat with you agreeing. You had to have your man and mine too. You always been greedy when it come to sex."

"Sista Willa! After all these years you're still upset about that night." Bertha said rolling her eyes. "Please. Let's not go through this again. You know them twins wasn't right and I'm just glad we found out about it when we did so we didn't waste time on them. Besides if they was any good I'd remember. Now where was we? Oh, yeah. I believe I asked you to stand up reverend so this ol' woman could see what you're working with."

"Lawdy! Lawdy! Lawdy! You always did have loose lips but you tellin' the truth about these here tickets. I could see spending two hundred and fifty dollars if we was going gambling and there was a show but I can sit at home n my front and watch niggas fuss and fight and act simple. We come to see some men and you the best we can do. And Bertha and me been wondering how the good Lord has really blessed so stand your ass up and let us take a peek."

"Stand on up," Bertha said in unison.

Wisdom who was in tears now could hardly catch his breath and stood to make his way to the bathroom.

"No one asked you to stand. Bertha said staring at Wisdom."

"Just need to use the bathroom if that's okay ma'am," he said apologetically.

"Why don't you get a picture or two of him? He ain't a bad lookin' man Sista Bertha."

"Ain't you been payin' attention? Wisdom here is married twice. He killed somebody and he a bigamist," she said loud enough for the whole bus to hear.

"What?! Chile you ain't serious. You sit next to some folks for years and never really know them."

"Sho is… Heard him tellin' the good reverend here just a few minutes ago. I be listenin'. My daddy useta always say if you want to learn ya gotta learn to listen."

"You ain't serious?"

"As a heart attack…"

"Lord! Lord! Lord!"

"Now that is one interesting piece of news but ya know I ain't opposed to a man being married more than once unless I was one of the women he was cheatin'on but

I ain't tryna marry no one so I don't know why that would make a difference to me. I just want a taste. Anybody that knows me knows I would prefer a married man if I had to have one cause I ain't the type of woman who wants somebody around all the time. And men tend to be *too* damn needy. They almost like children if you ast me. So, if he got a wife to tend to his needs all the better. Only thing I need 'em for is to scratch an occasional itch every now and then. And since I bought me a couple of them high intensity vibratin' stimulators I don't hardly need 'em for that."

"The devil's a lie. I ain't gonna sit here and try to pretend that I can go to the medicine cabinet and come back and satisfy myself like my man can. That's a bold faced lie. Ain't no substitutes for a good hard one going up in me."

"Ladies. Ladies," the good reverend said hoping to curtail the conversation although the bus seemed quite entertained by the two old women.

"Tell 'em sista." Butter chimed in. "There ain't no substitute for a man."

Willa shot Butter a quick smile before continuing.

"And like I told you before I's in pretty good condition. Got most of my teeth, ain't got no heart problems, no high blood pressures and 'cept for a little flab around the kitty I'm in great shape and good to go. An where that lil flab is concerned and aside from a few wrinkles here and there I just pull that to the side and it's all systems to go." Sista Willa said winking at the good reverend and Wisdom who had now returned.

The bus was pulling into the hotel parking lot now and an exasperated Reverend Goode breathed a deep sigh of relief. He could breathe a little easier now not having to worry about offending his two most loyal followers and found himself more than a lil ready to exit the bus.

Standing, Sista Bertha fumbled around in her purse frantically trying to find her camera and then pointing it in the direction of the good reverend.

"Not now Sister Bertha. Let's get situated. There will be plenty of time for that tonight."

"I certainly hope so reverend and don't forget you owe me and Sista Willa some quality time. And I mean some quality time. I don't think you want me to go and have a word with Ms. Goode requesting a lil of your time and tell he how you've been neglecting us poor ol' women and I don't think she'd appreciate that. Is that what I have to do reverend?"

"No. I don't think that will be necessary. I plan on making my rounds and making sure everyone is comfortable and settled in," the reverend said smiling cordially.

“I hear you reverend but I think I’m going to have a little chat with her anyway. How could she object? After all, she has you for three hundred and sixty five days of the year. All I’m asking for is a couple of hours. Young, vibrant thing that she is, I think she’ll understand,” Sista Bertha said smiling before patting the reverend lightly on his butt and sashaying away with Sista Willa.

“You serious? You gonna get you some time with that ain’tcha Bertha?”

“You damn skippy. I been fantasizing from the first pew for the last couple of years now. Ain’t missed a Sunday. I may be spiritual but I ain’t biblical and I plan on coveting ol’ girl’s husband if only for one night. I’m gonna let that young buck work the hell out of Ms. Kitty. That’s the good reverend’s job.”

“How you figure that?” Sista Willa asked somewhat confused.

"I want the good reverend to work the devil out of me," Bertha laughed.

"Umph. Umph, Umph. Girl how long we known each other?"

"Close to seventy years now. I ain't rightly sure. Why you ask?"

"Cause the more I get to know you the more I'm convinced all the loony's ain't in the bin. I always knew you weren't the brightest star up in the sky but please tell you how Ms. Goode a religious woman is going to just let you sleep with her husband?"

"Ain't I always told you to never underestimate Bertha Benjamin? If Bertha sets her sights on something you can best believe Bertha's gonna get it. This ain't just some hair brained scheme I just thought up. I've been planning this for close to a year now almost since our last retreat."

"Planning hell… Plotting and scheming is more like it. Some womens walkin' round here cryin' about how they needs and wants a man but not Bertha. I's been married and widowed four times. I'm financially set and could be married a fifth time if I seriously wanted to. If it's one thing I know its men. Funny thing I know women too. And that woman got her sights on faraway places. Oh, she married for appearances but her heart is elsewhere and she ain't got no problem letting me or anyone else have her husband cause she ain't really devoted to him. That I do know. Call it a women's intuition but I'm on point sista. You mark my words. This gonna be easy as pie you just watch and see." Bertha told a less than believing Willa.

Sista Willa had suspected dementia was setting in for some time now dropped her head and thought back to all the good times the two had shared over the years.

The good reverend stood in the center of the hotel lobby waiting patiently 'til everyone had assembled before addressing the boisterous crowd. Innocence kept a close eye on Hopeless who was now deep in the throes of withdrawal while Truth kept a wary eye out for Butter.

"Welcome all to A.M.E Zion's Third Annual Retreat. I hope all will find it a time of quiet introspection, prayer and Christian fellowship. We have a very loosely arranged itinerary which consists primarily of meals and a couple of workshops which I hope prove meaningful. Other than that you are on your own. We have two hours before dinner. You may want to check out the hotels amenities. I heard the pool and the Jacuzzi are to die for. There are also snowboarding, skiing and ATV trails for those of you inclined to outdoor activities. Or if you're like me you may just want to shower and relax. After dinner they'll be a small reception so you can all get to know each other a little better. Enjoy and I will see you at eight o'clock in banquet hall number three."

Two hours later the congregation adorned in their most elegant evening finery descended on the banquet hall.

Butter in a navy blue Jones of New York suit turned the most heads. Gone was the mascara and lip gloss. She wore no makeup and was absolutely stunning. Even Knowledge and the good reverend had to do a double take. Underneath all the gloss Butter was one beautiful woman.

Chicken, string beans and a baked potato were on the menu and everyone seemed to enjoy the cuisine—well that is everyone except Truth—who let her displeasure be known.

"You can tell White folks cooking. Ain't nobody cook string beans like White people. They're crunchy as hell and ain't got no taste whatsoever. They ain't do nothing but rinse them off and throw them on the plate like they garnish or something. And they call this fine dining. How hard is it to fry some damn fatback and throw an onion in for some damn seasoning?"

“They’re steamed,” Wisdom replied, “and actually better for you since steaming retains the nutrients.”

“That may be all well and good but it’s still bland and tasteless. And this chicken ain’t even fully cooked. Look there’s blood oozing from it. I can’t eat this shit,” Truth complained with her normal disgust before throwing her napkin into the plate.

Before Truth could utter another derogatory remark Butter had a handful of Truth’s dreadlocks and was bent over and whispering into her ear. All heads turned now remembering Butter’s early promise to beat Truth’s ass before the retreat was over.

“Listen missy, we are all here for one reason or another. We are supposing to be acting as good Christians and I swear fo’ God I’m trying but if I hear another negative thing outta yo’ mouth I’m gonna start whoopin’ your ass right there on the spot. Do you understand me? Now you pick up that form and pretend this is the best meal you ever tasted and don't you say another word this weekend. Do you hear me bitch?!" And with that Butter made her way back across the banquet hall and had a seat.

Truth picked up the fork never once looking and made short work of the remaining food on her plate without another word before excusing herself.

Everyone else seemed to enjoy the food and made quick work of it before finding their way to the reception area where they found wine and cheese as well as coffee and pastry for those that didn't imbibe.

The good reverend who was quite exhausted by this time found the strength to mingle among the small groups of parishioners. When he'd spoken to everyone and made his rounds he ultimately made his way to the sistas. Bertha spoke first.

"Where's the lovely Ms. Goode tonight reverend?"

"I'm afraid Ms. Goode isn't feeling too well this evening so I told her to skip dinner and the reception and get some rest. I'm sure she'll be good as new tomorrow."

"I reckon she will," Sista Bertha replied a sly grin stretching the many wrinkles on her face.

Meanwhile, in Room 307 the very attractive Ms. Goode bent over dragging the rather nattily attired middle-aged man's pants to his knees. When they were at his ankles she pushed him causing him to fall onto the loveseat naked from the waist down.

Standing she straddled him and lowered herself onto his already erect shaft. It had been years since she'd felt like this. With each rise and descent she took more of him into her until she engulfed all he had to offer. Stream of tears cascaded down her face but there was no sadness now. There was only joy for this is where she should have been.

"Oh, darling. It's been thirty years and I have never stopped loving you. How can you ever forgive me?"

"Shhh," he said gasping and unbuttoning Melinda's blouse. Little had changed and she was as full and firm as she had been when they were just kids in college and except for a few pounds around the mid-section she was every bit as fine as he'd remembered. But there was something different. He'd tried but had never gotten over her walking out on him with his best friend. He'd been here before though and feigned his passion. In reality he despised her.

Placing succulent kisses on her neck he watched as she melted beneath his touch gasping as a low moan escaped her lips. With gentle ease he lowered her bra straps letting her bra fall to the floor. Kissing her breasts he reached behind her and unzipped her skirt letting it fall to the floor as well. She had entered the hotel room full of passion and had assaulted him mounting him and riding him with reckless abandon letting loose all of the demons she had managed to keep hidden for far too long. Now that he had her fully disrobed it was his turn. To Melinda it took her back to their college days and she now knew she had made a mistake. She had not made love or felt love like this in twenty years not since she'd last been with him.

"My God I wish I could make you feel just how much I missed you. Every day for the past twenty years I've thought of this night; thought of the mistake I made and how I hurt you and it eats at me. I was so angry at you, angry that you couldn't find the time to spend with me."

"So, instead of coming to me and talking to me you took up with my best friend, my roommate and you slept with him, married him only to cheat on him as well. I have a hard time differentiating between you and Butter except that she's honest about being a whore."

"Is that what you think of me? Is that really all you think of me?" Melinda said screaming and bursting into tears. "After all these years that's what you think of me. I have never not once been unfaithful to Ben until now. And I was never unfaithful to you. You are the only two men I have ever loved and been with. How can you just call me a whore?"

"You cheated on me and now you're cheating on him."

"Oh K. know don't say that. You have to know I've always loved you," she was disgusting him now. "You know I'd go to the ends of the earth for you. I would do anything for you," she screamed as the tears flowed down her face. This admission did little to win favor in his eyes and he truly reviled the woman beneath him now.

"Is that right," he countered.

"You know I would K.," she said half pleading and grabbing at his still erect penis trying to guide it into her hot, throbbing sex.

Pulling away he stood up.

"Get on your knees."

Not knowing if he were serious or not she searched the deep recesses of his eyes almost pleading that he wasn't. Seeing no inclination Melinda sank to her knees.

"My God! K. please don't make me do this. I feel badly enough already. Take me with all the fervor and lust I know that you have always had for me. Show me how much you've missed me over the years. I've died a thousand deaths waiting and praying that you'd forgive me and would die a thousand more for your forgiveness. Tell me K. Please tell me what it is you want from me. Baby all I'm asking for is your forgiveness. I've carried this burden with me like a cancer for too long. It's eating at me. It's killing me. Can't you see the pain in my eyes, the burden in my heart? All I'm asking for is your forgiveness. Please tell me that you have the compassion in your heart to forgive. I need your forgiveness Knowledge. Baby I'd do anything!

Knowledge did not respond.

"Hush, Melinda. The time for talking has come and gone," he said zipping up his pants.

"Baby! No." Melinda said grabbing his leg and pulling him towards her and unzipping his pants and taking his now limber out. "If this is what you need to show you I love you and I'm sorry…" she said before closing her eyes and opening her mouth and sucking greedily.

It was impossible to know how many times he took her in the next hour but he was totally spent when he finally allowed her to leave. Her pelvic area was sore and bruised when he was finished. Melinda made her way gingerly to the door. She too was spent and although he'd finally forgiven her she hardly felt better leaving Knowledge's hotel room. Now she was confronted with brand new demons. How could she live with the infidelity to her husband?

Downstairs the reception was all but over. There were a few stragglers left behind including the good reverend who was exhausted and a bit tipsy thanks to Sista Bertha who seemed intent on getting the good reverend drunk and seducing with all her womanly wiles. After much prodding from the two elderly church members and an overwhelming sense of guilt the good reverend finally agreed to stop by the ladies room for a nightcap. Little did he know what lay in store. Somewhat concerned about Melinda who had made it an early exit complaining of sudden nauseousness the good reverend knew that a quick drink with the church's elders wouldn't take more than a few minutes and he could finally squash all their idle chatter about his not spending any time with them. For some reason though he felt uncommonly sleepy and fatigued almost as if he'd run a marathon. By the time they'd escorted him to their suite all the good reverend could do was fall out on the sofa. Trying to stand, Reverend Goode was surprised to find he couldn't. It was only then that the good reverend came to the realization that he may have been drugged. But who would do such a thing? His mind raced. He knew his congregation. They were after all his family. The more he tried to focus, to think, to recall anything out of the ordinary the more he drifted into a sea of oblivion.

"Sista Bertha! Sista Willa!"

"Yes reverend," Willa answered.

"I'm not sure what it is but I feel lightheaded. I think I'm coming down with whatever Ms. Goode has. You wouldn't mind if I take a few minutes to gather myself would you? I know it's getting late and you're probably tired but if you can just give me a few minutes."

"You take as long as you need reverend. I'll let Ms. Goode know of your whereabouts."

"Thank you sista," the good reverend said before closing his eyes.

When Bertha was quite sure the reverend was sound asleep she placed both arms under the two hundred pound man's armpits and dragged him into the bedroom and onto the king sized bed.

"How you makin' out in there?"

"Boy weighs a ton but I can manage. You go and take care of the missus. Once she's out of the way we can do with him as we damn well please. Just sit with her for a little while 'til she gets sleepy then tuck her in. You got the tea? Drop a tab or two in her tea and she should be out for the night."

"You sure about this Bertha? It don't hardly seem right."

"Let me worry about what's right. Or would you prefer sittin' up half the night with ol' man Barnes. How long has you been waitin' for that ol' geezer to give you some. You steady up there wastin' money at Victoria's Secret and it's still a secret to ol' man Barnes," Bertha laughed. "It's the same thing every Friday; week in and week out. He comin' over. You feedin' him and getting' all sexy and what he do when it's doin' time? Not a goddurn thing. Nothing. Ol' fool gets to droolin' and the next you know he's snorin' and falls asleep and you still wishin' and hopin' and still burnin' up with them there feelin's. And all you gets is to wake him up and shoo him home. And you on fire."

"You right. I cain't argue with you there."

"I know I'm right. Now go ahead and put the reverend's wife to bed. While you're doing that I'm going to break the good reverend in right nice. By the time you get back I'll have him up again, primed and ready to go. Now git, woman. "

"Alright! Alright! I swear you sho is gittin' ornery and cantankerous in your old age."

"Am not. I just knows what I need and I ain't got time to discuss it. I know when I's doin' time. Now would you please handle your bizness so's I can handle mine."

"Oh alright heifer." Willa said closing the door behind her.

Bertha arose from the Queen Anne chair and winked at Sista Willa on her way to the bathroom. Removing her clothes she stepped into the shower and allowed the warm waters to caress her gently. She was ready. When she was finished she threw on the floral house dress she wore on just such occasions and proceeded back to the living room to find the good reverend sound asleep and snoring lightly. Shaking him and getting little response other than a slight moan the old woman smiled.

"You just right reverend," the woman who could have passed for an aging Lena Horne grinned.

"Just the way I like my men. Strong and silent," she said pulling the straps from her shoulders and letting the long flowing dress fall to the ground. Completely naked now she reached for the glass of water from the nightstand and placed her dentures there.

"Trust me reverend. When I get finished with you you gonna know you married the wrong woman," she said turning off the light before bending over him and taking his limp member in her mouth and sucking tenderly.

Minutes later, a deep smile etched from the good reverend' face each time her lips found the tip.

"I believe you're ready," the woman grinned as she stroked his granite hard penis. Bertha stood up, threw one leg over the good reverend, straddling him guiding him into the deep, warm recesses of her throbbing vagina. When she had taken all of him she gasped and grinned widely.

"You're a big one fo' sho'. God done really blessed you she said easing down slowly. Woo Lord! You're a big one but Bertha ain't had one she can't take. Lord knows I'm gonna be sore for a week but goodness it sure feels good now," she muttered lost in her own euphoria. "I don't know if Willa's gonna be able to handle all of this," bertha smiled.

After riding the good reverend with reckless abandon she felt herself coming to a shuddering orgasm.

Spent she bent over sweat dripping took the good reverend in her hands and massaged him until he was hard again. Hard almost immediately, Bertha grinned.

"That was quick reverend. I'm thinking Ms. Goode must not be taking care of her wifely duties but don't you worry reverend I'll be your angel tonight. This time she rode him slow and methodically feeling each and every stroke. She closed her eyes now and dreamed. If there was a heaven she hardly knew how it could be any better. His eyes were open now. Suddenly realizing what was happening to him he tried to grab her but was unable to move. His arms tied he felt helpless.

"Sista Bertha, please. Please untie me. Please don't do this. Please..."

"You ain't got to beg rev. I know the pussy's good but you ain't got to beg rev. Sista Bertha gonna give you enough to tide you over."

"No, Bertha! No!"

"No what baby. Are you trying to tell me you don't want no more of Sista Bertha's sweet pussy? Are you trying to tell me my pussy don't feel good to you?"

The good reverend could hardly say that but how could he condone such a thing. And he couldn't lie. The woman knew how to work it. Still, he knew the devil took many forms.

"Sista Bertha," he said before gasping.

"Good ain't it reverend," she laughed. The tears rolled down the good reverend's face. He couldn't remember the last time he'd been loved so good or felt such passion in his loins. He couldn't remember the last time he had enjoyed sex.

"Sista Bertha," he yelled.

"Yes, baby."

She was playing with him now, toying with him, teasing him, barely letting him enter her lowering herself down only enough to let him place the head inside of her before pulling away. His back arched in an attempt to fully penetrate her only to have her pull away.

"Sista Bertha," he cried.

"Tell me you want it," she said grinning now. She knew she had hm.

"Please."

"Please what? Didn't have time for me before. Bet you'll have time from now on won't you rev? Next time Sista Bertha asks for a little time you'll find the time won't you rev? The way I see it I'm free after Bingo and bible studies on Wednesday nights. Is that good for you rev?"

"Sista Bertha you know I'm married."

"And you point is? You know the saying? What happens with Bertha stays with Bertha. I see no point in telling her. Do you? 'Sides how you gonna explain you fuckin' a seventy-four year old senior citizen. But the truth is you she don't make you feel like this in bed do she? You don't get to be this ol' bein' no fool and Bertha can see that though she loves you and cares about you she ain't in love with you. Ain't that the truth boy?' Bertha said moving off him and reaching for a cigarette. "Ain't no love therefore ain't no passion."

The good reverend turned his head away from the old woman. He knew she was right.

"Enjoy the moment rev. Tonight I want you to forget the idea that you're the shepherd chosen to take care of his flock. Let your demons go and indulge a lonely woman. Indulge yourself. You're allowed some happiness and I'm going to make sure you have it for your sake and for mine. Now work with me," she said as she swallowed his now limp penis and sucked it 'til he was hard again and then rode it again until both came to a screaming climax.

"Thank you Reverend Goode. Thanks for indulging an old woman in a minor frivolity," Bertha said as she wiped the reverend clean with a warm wash rag. "And should you get a notion to, feel free o stop by on Wednesdays after bible study. I'd really like that," she said smiling as she pulled on her cigarette.

"I may just do that Sista Bertha. Now may I go? I'm sure my wife is probably worried sick about me."

"C'mon rev. You know better than that. And I would say yes but my girl ain't had none in a minute and I promised her."

"You're not serious!"

"Oh, but I am. Besides outside of being a little on the plump side and homely as hell she's a beautiful person and truly in need. Do her some justice and give her a little. I promised her I'd save her some and I promise you it won't take much."

"Okay Sista Bertha. This has gone far enough. I agreed to meet you. And perhaps a lot of what you say is true but even if I were to meet you at the risk of losing my job and my wife I refuse to let you blackmail or coerce me to sleep with whomever whenever you get ready. If you want to do some ministry or missionary work for all the old and lonely lost souls out there that's fine but I will not be the tool in which you use to do it with. Do you understand me? I am not the one. However you deem to seem my marriage the fact is that I am married. I took a vow under the Lord's eye and I will not break it because of some carnal lust you and Sista Willa have. I am being held against my will which in any court of the land is tantamount to kidnapping."

"I wonder how that will stand up in court when Sista Willa and I take stand. Imagine two seventy four year old women kidnapping and raping a strong virile fifty year old man. I sincerely doubt that a jury will hardly see two elderly senior citizens, two loyal, church-going women like Willa and myself holding you hostage and raping you. They'd laugh you right out of the court and if you ever thought of proposing the idea you would only put doubt in the eyes of every church member who hides you in such high esteem let alone Ms. Goode. How will your marriage be after that little scandal?"

The good reverend a man of rather good judgment let the idea fester for a minute before speaking.

"Sista Bertha, I will forget this event ever happened if you let me up now. Either that or I will take my chances in a court of law."

Before the good reverend could utter another word the old woman leaned over grabbed one of her fishnet stockings and stuffed as much as she could in the good reverend's mouth. Back on top she was coming now for the third time. Hard and fast and ten just as quickly as it began it was over. Sista Bertha rolled over next to the good reverend took a cigarette from her pack and lit it pulling slowly.

"I do believe I'd pay for some more of that. That was the best I've had in quite some time," she said smiling contentedly. "Ain't often a man can satisfy me but I gotta admit you get the job done. Not sure if the role playing had anything to d with it or not but I'm still getting the chillies. If Sista Willa don't get here soon I may have to take her turn to," the old laughed.

The good reverend was too exhausted to say anything. Seeing this Bertha removed the stocking from his mouth.

"May I assume I'll see you on Wednesday or are you still taking me to court."

When the reverend declined to answer the old woman continued.

"You were so talkative earlier. Now nothing. I'll have to assume that's a yes and maybe we can role play again although I think we may want to change the scenario for your sake," she said laughing heartily. "Maybe we can reverse the roles. I've never had a man forcibly take me and believe it or not I can be submissive," she said chuckling before going to the bathroom and washing up. Returning the old woman brought a warm rag and gently washed the good reverend's private parts.

"I gots to give it to you rev, Ms. Goode is one lucky woman. I've had a few lovers in my day but for me to have an orgasm is almost unheard of. But to have four one right after another is hard for even me to believe. I ain't got no qualms about paying my tithes and I must say that in all of the twenty years of attending and listening to you preach I have to admit this is without a doubt the best service I've attended so far. Lord knows all your talent ain't reserved for the pulpit. No sooner had she finished giving her thanks and praises than she heard the hotel door close.

"Play along reverend. You know how Sista Willa is. Gals always been a little skittish. I told her I'd have you primed and ready to go so you be still and let's see how much you have left," she said adjusting he dress before bending over and sucking him lightly. In a matter of seconds the good reverend was at full attention.

"Damn I sho' could go for some more of you rev. I hope it's one and done and she carries her big ass to sleep so I can have another go at you," Bertha commented before kissing the good reverend on the forehead. "Thank you reverend for giving an old lady just what she needed. Now close our eyes rev. You know the gal's a basket case. She find out you're conscious she may just go into cardiac arrest. Now hush and close our eyes.

Willa is that you?"

"Yeah, it's me," Willa said sticking her head in the door. Oh my! Is he awake? You said he'd be out cold Bertha. Lord. Lord. Lord. I don't know why I let you talk me into your hair-brained schemes. Here we are two old ladies going to jail for kidnapping and rape and not just any old rape but raping a man of the cloth, a minister to boot. They sho' nuff gonna throw the book at us this time Bertha."

"Oh hush Willa. The good reverend ain't gonna say shit and even if he did who gonna believe that two old ladies in their seventies took advantage of a big, ol' strappin' buck like Reverend Goode. It ain't even feasible. And speaking of big he hung real heavy. Scared me at first. Broke my back tryna handle all of that. Ripped my innards up but Lord knows it was good going down. Give me just a second and let me get him primed for you. Why don't you go freshen up in the meantime and grab some of that K-Y jelly out of my overnight bag? Trust me you gonna need it. The good reverend is rather well-endowed. He's got my shit on fire! Probably be a day or two before I can walk straight but it was so good I made him promise me he gonna cripple me again on Wednesday after bible study."

"And he agreed?"

"Well, you know he ain't the only one here that's blessed. And after a taste of this how's he just gonna walk away? After five husbands don't you think I know how to please a man? He may be holy and sanctified in the morning but by the time the evening rolls in Bertha go him sinnin' and signin' his soul away," Bertha laughed. "How he gonna experience this and then just walk away. Now what you waitin' for gal? I got him up and ready to go. Come on sista! It's doin' time. I'm going down to the bar and get me a stiff one so you can have a little privacy. Be back in an hour."

"You think I should? I mean I really haven't participated in anything so I haven't committed any crime."

Bertha didn't even bother to answer knowing that her hormones were raging it was just a moot point and all she could do was chuckle and feel for the good reverend under Willa's watch.

The good reverend tried to shake his head but the long in Willa's eyes let him know that his words would only fall on deaf ears.

Now if ever there were a good cop bad cop scenario this was it. And hearing the hotel door close Willa didn't even bother to freshen up and after securing the lock on the front door headed straight for the reverend.

Willa was a pretty woman, always had been. Her curse was that she was big, standing close to six four and weighing close to two hundred and fifty pounds she presented quite an imposing figure towering over most of the men she came into contact with. But not tonight, tonight she was going to exorcise her demons. There was no pretense, no lingerie from Victoria's Secret. No tonight she had a captive audience.

The good reverend who saw this last tryst as a foregone conclusion gasped when he saw this Amazon of a woman approach the bed dressed only in heels.

"My God woman," he yelled forgetting the promise to Sista Bertha. "Please don't do this. It's a sin against God and man."

"I'm so sorry reverend. I can only hope that my God is a forgiving God," Willa said as she mounted the good reverend. "Now you just be a good boy and relax. Willa ain't greedy. I just need one good one and I'll let you be."

Pulling the covers down to the foot of the bed, Willa gasped.

"Sista ain't never lied about you," she said smiling as she eased down on the good reverend. It was the last time there was anything easy about the encounter as she slammed her two hundred and fifty pounds down onto the man beneath her each time with more force. Two minutes later an exhausted Willa rolled over with a smile on her face.

The good reverend stared up at the ceiling. His mind fought the drugs and alcohol as he tried to make sense of it all. Sista Bertha had been right. His marriage was a farce. Sure, he loved Melinda but neither had been able to get over Knowledge's betrayal. And in twenty years neither had felt comfortable enough to bring it up but it hadn't taken him long to realize that although she loved and cared about him it was no more than that simply a symbiotic relationship they shared and he was sure that she wasn't and had never been in love with him. It was simply a matter of convenience and security. And with all his work with the church it was easy to overlook this tiny flaw which offered no solace at the end of a long day. He'd often been tempted to creep out on her but the women he knew were all in some way connected to the church and plotting to see who could depose the first lady so he'd refrained. Perhaps a little Wednesday night bible study to help Sista Bertha wasn't out of the realm of possibilities. Older and more mature than most she wanted no parts of being the wife of a minister or anybody else for that matter and the mere age difference would in itself negate any suspicion. He smiled through the pain in his loins and seriously considered the older woman's proposition.

Moments later, still wrapped up in his thoughts he heard the door close.

"Sista Willa. Are you okay?"

Getting no response Bertha peeked in the bedroom then laughed.

"I tried to tell her she was in over her head reverend but she's always been hardheaded and stubborn. Thanks for taking care of her though. I know she needed that. How you feeling?"

"I'm okay sista."

"You have enough energy to take a sista around the world one last time?"

"Only if you untie me and let me show you how it's done."

"You're serious? You're not just saying that so you can run?"

"Sista Bertha you're going to have to let me go eventually. Trust me you have my word."

"I guess if you can't trust a man of the cloth who can you trust?"

Bertha untied the good reverend's hands and stepped back. He rubbed his wrists with the rope had left a nasty burn. He then got up and in one fell swoop he grabbed Sista Bertha up in his arms and carried her into the living room where he laid her on the couch. Shocked she stared into his eyes trying to read this man not knowing what to expect. She didn't have to wait long.

"Turn over sista."

"Like this?" she said her ass sticking up in the air.

"Just like that," the reverend countered before spitting on his hand then lubricating his member before slamming it into the elderly woman.

"Is this what you want?" He asked slamming it in harder and harder as far as he could.

"Oh, God yes. I'm coming reverend."

The elderly woman came two or three times before the good reverend was finished.

"My God that was good rev," Sista Bertha said as she lit another cigarette and reached for the fifth of Chivas Regal and poured herself two fingers. "I want to thank you for blessing me. I doubt that I will see you anymore this weekend. I got everything I came for tonight. I only hope that you'll see fit to revisit this very same spot on Wednesday night. Nothing like a little physical therapy to keep a gal spry and agile you know," Bertha said grinning widely.

"There's a very distinct possibility of that. And thank you for awakening the passion in me. I'd forgotten what it was. You opened my eyes to some things that I hadn't wanted to confront but there's no need living a lie. Now the next thing to do is to confront the issue."

"I hope I didn't cause any real problems."

"The problems have always been there. I just chose to ignore them but no longer does that seem possible especially now."

"Glad to have helped rev."

The reverend was fully dressed by this time and as he checked his tie he bent over and kissed the old woman deeply and passionately despite her not having her teeth in then headed for the front door.

"Is Wednesday the only day you're free?"

"I'm free for you any time you want to minister rev," Bertha said grinning sheepishly.

Glancing out the door the good reverend was surprised to find a small crowd gathered at the end of the hall at the stairwell. Most were members of his congregation with a few stragglers mixed in.

"What's going on," he asked Wisdom.

"Don't know. I just got here but it seems to be some commotion coming from the bottom of the stairs. I can't get close enough to see."

The reverend's mind raced. The church had reserved two floors in the luxury hotel for the retreat and although it didn't have to be one of the congregation there was a good chance it just could be. He hoped no one had fallen or fallen sick. Moving toward the stairwell he became acutely aware that whoever it was no one seemed to be concerned enough to lend a hand. Moving closer he began to make out the voices.

"Bitch there 's always one. There's always one to say some shit and get her ass beat. Now tell me if it was worth this ass whooping girlfriend."

By the time the good reverend could get to the top of the stairwell everything came into focus. Butter had waited until Truth had left the reception before following her up the stairs. Catching her in the secluded stairwell she'd grabbed the petite young lady and began pummeling her until Truth in an attempt to defend off he blows had fallen to the ground, balled up into the fetal position and scream for help.

Most of the church congregation had come but not to her rescue. It was obvious that they thought she was receiving her just due and stood idly by while Butter beat and berated Truth.

"I thought activists were fighters. You may be an activist but you sure as hell ain't no fighter. Now get the hell up. Stomping yo' ass is fuckin' up my Menolo's bitch."

The good reverend parted the onlookers and finally made it to the lower landing. He was exhausted but finally managed to harness Butter's rage and pull her off the now semi-conscious woman.

"Some of you men grab he and take her to my room," the good reverend shouted. Hopeless grabbed her under her armpits while Wisdom who'd followed the good reverend grabbed her feet and took her downstairs to the reverend's suite.

"I can't believe you good, church people would just stand around and let this girl get pummeled."

"That big mouthed, hatin' bitch got what she deserved," someone shouted out from the back of the crowd."

"It was just a matter of time before somebody stomped a mud hole in her ass," someone else chimed in.

"You may be right but who are we to judge?" the good reverend replied.

"We ain't judge reverend. Butter Love did that along with passing sentence and prosecutin' her dumb ass too," someone else said causing the crowd to break out in laughter.

Reverend Goode knew it was hopeless. They'd been drinking and Truth's random attacks on anyone in sight during the bus ride didn't sit well with anyone. Now as promised she had paid and paid dearly.   The doctor reported her as having a minor concussion and two broken ribs.

Ms. Goode, the reverend's loyal wife spent the remainder of the night caring for the young woman and if it hadn't been for her own splitting headache she probably wouldn't have minded a bit. At least now she wouldn't have to confess her infidelity to her husband while she waited for him to pass judgment, sentence and banish her.

He too was glad that his wife was preoccupied. He had issues of his own and knew when he left Bertha that the marriage was over and all that was left was for him to man up and ask for a divorce. He dreaded the thought but knew it was avoidable. It after all had been a long time in coming but after tonight he knew that he could no longer share a bed with her. Nor did he want to.

During the following day activities the church members took turns caring for Truth who had suddenly grown quite humble apologetic. These same people she'd called hypocrites and lost sheep with no direction not more than twenty four hours ago were now the ones she was depending on to empty her bed pan. They visited her on their trysts around the hotel bringing her flowers, magazines and food. And all the attention and caring she received from these lazy, no-good apathetic Black folk she'd condemned earlier made her sit back and reflect.

And then in the presence of the good reverend she received the most unlikely of visitors. Butter love walked into the bedroom accompanied by the good reverend.

"It's okay Truth. Butter has assured me that she's just here to apologize."

And with that he closed the door and left the two women to work out their grievances with Butter's assurance that she wouldn't finish the job.

"Damn girl. It looks like someone spanked that ass pretty damn good. I'm thinking you must have really offended someone but then I'm sure you working on behalf of Black folks wouldn't purposely offend your own folk. But then I'm thinking that you must have from the size of that shiner. And I have to ask myself that with all your proclaiming to be working on behalf of us poor, lazy apathetic, good for nothing Black folks not one of them would lend you a hand when you was getting' your ass trashed last night." Butter said digging through her pocketbook. Truth cringed and was about to scream for the good reverend when Butter pulled up on her cigarettes and lighter. Seeing the petrified look on Truth's face Butter had to smile.

"Don't worry baby girl. I just came here to talk. Real talk. The good reverend thinks I came to apologize and that's fine but Butter don't apologize for being insulted. Sorry baby girl but nowhere in my bible does it say turn the other cheek. And it's a good bible. My bible says an eye for an eye. You feel me? I think you do from the looks of you. But what I really came to tell you and before last night you saw yourself as some highfalutin' queen of the Africans with us being some lonely good for nothings that didn't know their ass from their belly button. You couldn't see, couldn't hear until you fell and hit your head. Not you're bruised and beat up. It's a hard way to learn but from my perspective it's what I call an optimum teaching moment. So, here's your lesson for today and if you're smart you'll take this with you and use it if no other reason than to avoid getting your ass spanked again.

You see everyone has their own foundation, their own experience that help them come to be who they are. Who's to say who's right and who's wrong? It certainly isn't you or I and everyone has their own road to travel. Some may take a lifetime to get where you already are. You may take the road less traveled and arrive early while the rest of us take the crowded and congested one. In the end it's all good. The point is we are all travelling. I see you're not following me or perhaps you're preoccupied with the idea that I'm going to jump up out of this chair and finish the job I started last night. I'm not so stop your worrying. But let me share with you something shared with me a long time ago when I was like you. I ran in and tried to force my thoughts, my ideas and values on them. I was ranting and raving because I knew I knew. I was enlightened. I had the answers and they were grasping for straws in the dark. When I'd finished my whole diatribe on the secrets of the universe the man sat there smiling at me and all he said to me was 'that every man finds their God in their own time'. I have never forgotten those words or that man. He was my father. I saw him twice in my life but I will never forget those words.

I'm gonna leave you with that and I hope it does you some good. It may even save you an ass whoopin'. And whether you know it or not your ideas and opinions are only important to you baby girl. That's real talk." And with that Butter grabbed her purse turned and walked out the door.

Innocence was enjoying herself. She'd gone to a couple of workshops, spent some time in the pool and Jacuzzi and even convinced Hopeless to try skiing and riding ATV's over the countless trails. She couldn't remember having so much fun. Now as she sat pouring over schoolwork while Hopeless sat there skimming through a SLAM magazine she couldn't help but wonder what would transpire when they got back home. Sure she had male friends and yes Hopeless had her by nine years. Yet, despite his addiction and his constant throwing up she found they had more in common than almost anyone she knew. Easy to laugh, he was bright and spontaneous and just fun to be with. Since their little dust up they had been virtually inseparable. And in less than twenty four hours it would all be over or would it. Hopeless was right in a way and she'd been offended. It was true. Her parents had done everything to isolate and protect her from the ills of society but being on this bus trip brought her to the sudden realization that there was so much more to the world than what they presented to her. She had a chance to hear the world from a side she'd never known, felt compassion for a man down on his luck who she'd first thought to be worthless. She could now empathize with those other than herself and wasn't sure if she was falling in love.

Innocence closed the book. She could no longer concentrate.

"Hopeless, I want you to do something for me."

"Anything baby."

"I want you to meet me in my room in about fifteen minutes."

"Okay. But can I ask what this is all about?"

"Just meet me there. I have to stop by and check on Truth. Give me a few minutes."

A voracious reader Hopeless took the textbook from Innocence leafed through it until he found a short story by Langston Hughes to his liking and eagerly devoured it.

Fifteen minutes later Hopeless knocked on the door as instructed. Innocence appeared just as he'd seen her in the lobby only something was different. Still dressed in the blue and gold North Carolina Aggies sweat suit and blue Nike Air Max he gazed at her.

"Come in and have a seat."

"What is it that you wanted to talk t me about and that you couldn't talk to me about that you couldn't talk to me about downstairs?"

"Hopeless. I've never been one to beat around the bush so I'm going to be brutally honest with you. When you got on the bus I really thought you were rather ratchet but as I came to know you I had to admit I couldn't have been more wrong. The more I got to know you the more I came to like you. I was downstairs trying to study but couldn't focus wondering what was going to happen when this retreat was over. Would I see you again? I think I'm in love with you Hopeless and if we don't ever get a chance to cross paths again I want to have something to remember you by. So, I want you to make love to me."

Hopeless' head jerked up. He was speechless. There was no doubt she was as cute as she could be. And there was little doubt that he felt the same way.

"I thought about that too. Not the part about me making love but the possibility of us going back to our comfy little coffins and not seeing each other again. It's not a pleasant thought especially since I'm crazy about you as well. But now that we have that established we can exchange numbers and make it a point to stay in touch."

Innocence was all aglow with this recent admission.

"And I'm not saying that I don't find you crazy attractive but how long have we known each other? Two days? Let's talk about that again after six months. Let's make sure."

Innocence grabbed Hopeless and kissed him softly but passionately.

"You just picked up a bushel of brownie points."

"I need to talk to you Melinda."

"I need to talk to you as well," the good reverend said staring at the table settings before them as they shared the final meal of the retreat.

In the end they agreed that a divorce was imminent and long overdue. They hugged warmly as if each had found relief in the fact that their union was over.

The bus ride home was just the opposite of the ride there and it appeared that everyone in attendance had come to an epiphany of sorts.